The Reluctant Vampire

ERIC MORECAMBE

It is a wild, stormy night in the small village of Katchem-by-the-Throat, in the tiny country of Gotcha, where the unhappy Gots are still ruled by Vampires after four hundred years. At Bloodstock Castle lives Victor, King of the Vampires, and his devoted wife, Queen Valeeta. They have two sons: Vernon, who has a nasty habit of turning people into stone, and Valentine, who reveals the horrible fact that he can't stand the taste of blood! That's only the beginning of an incredible story that will keep readers of all ages in stitches!

ERIC MORECAMBE

The
Reluctant Vampire

Illustrated by Tony Ross

MAMMOTH

This book is dedicated to

Steven James Bartholomew
Julian Gibbs
Ian Cockhill
Kingsley Roberts
Tom Barnes
and Darcey Cohill

Their knowledge of Vampires and their habits was
invaluable.

First published in Great Britain 1982
by Methuen Children's Books Ltd
Magnet edition published 1983
Reprinted 1984, 1985, 1986 and 1987
Published 1990 by Mammoth
an imprint of Mandarin Paperbacks
Michelin House, 81 Fulham Road, London SW3 6RB

Mandarin is an imprint of the Octopus Publishing Group

Text copyright © 1982 Eric Morecambe
Illustrations copyright © 1982 Tony Ross

ISBN 0 7497 0315 6

A CIP catalogue record for this title
is available from the British Library

Reproduced, printed and bound in Great Britain by
BPCC Hazell Books
Aylesbury, Bucks, England
Member of BPCC Ltd.

Contents

CHAPTER 1

*Valentine arises,
As Dr Plump advises.*

It was January in the year of seventeen ninety-nine. The sky was as wet and as black as a bottle of ink. A shaft of blue lightning suddenly lit up the seven-hundred-year-old castle on top of a hill. Small yellow lights flickered from behind a barred window in the highest room of the highest turret. For a few seconds before the lightning went out, the castle was silhouetted against thick, huge clouds, fat with rain. The wind bent double the tallest trees on the hill. They almost creaked with pain. The moon could occasionally be seen flying through the clouds at what seemed an incredible speed. Suddenly, it threw a few seconds of yellow light on to a thin ribbon of road leading up to the drawbridge of the silent castle.

On the road was a small coach being pulled by a

1

very frightened horse. The driver was Doctor Plump. Although his name was Plump, he was the thinnest man you could ever imagine. He was six feet six inches tall but when he wore his top hat he was seven feet six inches tall, and when he was on horseback he was well over ten feet tall.

Doctor Plump was a humourless man with lips as thin as a grasshopper's legs. A large Roman nose – almost large enough for a Roman to sit on – hung between his small, piggy eyes. His eyes were so deep set in his head they looked as if they had been put there with a Black and Decker.

He had been summoned to the castle urgently. His poor horse was wet through with rain and perspiration. The fear showed in its eyes as they rolled round faster than an old woman's birthday. Doctor Plump urged the animal forward with the snap of a long whip that stung the horse like an injection from a blunt syringe, and they sped towards their goal, Bloodstock Castle, overlooking the small village of Katchem-by-the-Throat in the tiny mid-European country of Gotcha.

The 'Gots' were an unhappy people with no king of their own or even a president to rule them. They were ruled by the Vampires of Bloodstock Castle and had been for the past four hundred years.

The horse clattered over the wooden drawbridge as it took the carriage and Doctor Plump inside the courtyard. The Doctor pulled the horse to a halt, jumped off the coach and with his black doctor's bag in his hand, ran towards the massive iron and wooden door, leaving the tired, bewildered horse covered in a cloud of hot steam.

He pulled hard on an iron bar with a handle

attached. A bell sounded inside the castle loud enough to awaken the dead and their friends, the undead, who are like their dead friends but can come back to life again.

Dr Plump waited, wrapping his long, black scarf closer around his thin, scrawny neck. The echo of the bell died down and then the only sound was the rain hitting his top hat as loud as the chattering teeth of an Eskimo with flu.

From inside, the Doctor heard bars being drawn to allow the great door to be opened. It opened, but no more than a crack. He looked into the one black eye of Igon.

Igon was as ugly as it was possible to be. In fact, uglier. He had only one eye, hence the name Igon. A glass eye hung round his neck in a pouch but he only used it on certain occasions such as reading the paper. He would sometimes put it in his trouser pocket to see how much money he had left.

The Doctor spoke.

'Doctor Plump,' he wheezed.

'No, I'm not. I'm Igon,' said Igon and slammed the door.

The Doctor was left in the pouring rain, the driving wind and the dark night. He thumped as hard as he could on the great iron door.

'Igon!' he shouted against the door and the wind.

'Who is it?' said a voice from the other side of the door.

'Doctor Plump,' the wet doctor shouted.

'He's not here,' Igon shouted back.

'No. *I'm* Plump.'

'You should go on a diet then,' said Igon, who wasn't the cleverest person in the world.

3

'Please, I'm Doctor Plump.' He put his mouth closer to the door. 'I've been summoned.'

After a second or two the iron bars were once again removed from their sockets and the door creaked open a little. The same, single, black eye peered out.

The Doctor spoke very quickly. 'I'm Doctor Plump and His Most Gracious Vampari, King Victor, sent for me to have a look at His Serene Vampary Prince Valentine.'

The door opened slowly. 'Come in,' Igon said gruffly.

The Doctor walked in with one long stride. Igon shut the door. Doctor Plump looked around the large hall. It was very dimly lit with no fire to help dry his wet clothes or furniture on which to lay his top hat and overcoat; it was just a very large, very high, freezing cold castle.

The Doctor looked down at Igon. He saw a small, twisted body with a hideous face. His back was bent double with the weight of a large hump that made him walk with his left shoulder nearer to the ground than his right one. His clothes (if you could call them that) were rags. Igon looked up as the Doctor looked down. Igon smiled, showing a most beautiful set of gums.

'Follow me.' He slid along the floor away from the door. 'This way, please, Doctor Pump.'

'Plump,' the Doctor checked. 'Doctor Plump.'

'That's what I said, Pump. I have great difficulty saying my 'l's as I have no teeth, so saying difficulty was even more difficult for me than saying Plump, Doctor Pump.' Igon shuffled towards some distant steps.

The Doctor, a little nonplussed, followed behind him. He tried to make a little light conversation.

4

'It's a wild night.'

'What do you expect for July?'

'But it's January,' the Doctor said in a small, surprised voice.

'I'll bet it gets worse in August,' Igon snarled. The Doctor looked mystified.

They had by now reached the steps, which spiralled round a huge wall like a vine round a tree. The steps were no more than eighteen inches wide, with no handrail. One side of the steps clung to the wall, on the other side was an empty space. One slip and you could fall to the stone flags below and be given a rather large collection of broken ribs. The safest way to climb them was slowly and carefully and to keep one open-palmed hand almost glued to the wall for support. The Doctor nervously followed Igon.

Igon's bent body found great difficulty in climbing the steps, taking at least half a minute to move from one to the next. The Doctor, following Igon, looked up at all the steps they still had to climb and worked out quickly in his mind that at the rate Igon was climbing they would both be forty-five minutes older by the time they reached the top.

'Do you think that maybe I should go first?' the Doctor asked courteously, trying not to offend the bent, broken body in front of him.

'No,' came the painfully grunted reply. 'We'll rest for a while.'

'Rest?' the Doctor questioned. 'Rest?' Good Lord, we've only walked up five steps.'

'You may have only walked up five steps but, my long thin friend, I've climbed them. We shall rest.'

Igon sat on the sixth step trying to get his breath. The Doctor stood towering over him and watched.

After two minutes of gasping and heavy bronchial breathing, Igon slowly took his glass eye out, spat on it and quickly rubbed it with one of the rags he was wearing. He held it in front of him between his thumb and first finger and said, 'It gets darker as we go higher.'

Eventually, they reached the top of the stairs and on the landing they saw the door leading into the unliving quarters of the Vampire King and Queen, Prince Valentine and Valentine's brother, Prince Vernon.

Vernon was mean and hateful. He was the least liked in the family. He was also the elder of the two brothers.

The Doctor waited for Igon to knock on the door. As this didn't happen, he said slowly and with a touch of annoyance:

'Are you going to knock or have you got a key?'

'It's no good knocking. The rooms where they reside are at least another five minutes' walk along the corridors.'

'I see,' the Doctor said with a forced calm. 'So I presume that you have a key to get us past this massive door?' He gave Igon a stiff grin.

'Of course,' said Igon nervously.

'Well?' the Doctor asked.

'Yes I am, thank you. I'm very well, considering,' Igon smiled once more to the Doctor.

'Pardon?' questioned the Doctor, trying to work out the conversation.

'What?' said Igon, not letting his eye look straight at the Doctor's.

'What do you mean, what?' asked the Doctor, who in spite of the cold was beginning to lose his cool.

6

'What do you mean, what do you mean? Eh? What?' Igon was playing for time. The Doctor started to twitch, first his eye, then his bottom lip. He was getting almost to the exasperated stage. Self-control was more difficult to find. His temper was starting to show. You could always tell when his temper was ready to get the better of him. It was then that he started to crack his knuckles. Unfortunately, he was cracking them on Igon's head.

'The key. Where's the key, you curled up lout?' he whispered viciously.

'On the table,' Igon replied in a hurt voice.

'Which table?' the Doctor asked with controlled hysteria.

Igon pulled himself up to an almost upright position and with his gnarled hand pointed down the steps, and, with a dignity that any monarch would be proud of, said, 'On the table, sir. The one in the kitchen.'

The matchstick-thin Doctor suddenly burst into tears; uncontrollable, fast-flowing tears that ran from his eyes like two small rivers in flood and about to burst their banks.

Igon was fascinated. He had never seen two eyes cry before. He had only ever seen one eye cry and that was his own when his mother used to hit him for being ugly, which was every day. Then he would look in the mirror at his one crying eye. He cried because he was so very ugly, not because of the pain inflicted by his mother's heavy hand.

He would look in that mirror and wonder why he was so very ugly and ask his reflection 'Why am I so ugly?' . . . 'No one is ever going to love me. No one is ever going to want me as their friend. I'm going to go through life always being lonely. I'm so ugly even *I* wouldn't want to be friends with me.' And he would watch a tear roll down from his eye.

Then, taking his glass eye out of his pocket, he would look at it and wonder why it didn't cry. After all, it was an eye; his eye. But poor Igon was never told it wasn't an eye at all. It was only a blue glass marble that had been in a Christmas cracker which he'd stolen and pulled. He pulled it alone as no-one wanted to share a cracker, let alone Christmas, with him and, of course, he was fascinated when the eye (as he thought) dropped out. As far as Igon was concerned, it was Heaven's work.

By now the half-crazed Doctor had grabbed Igon and was shaking him with a fierceness and strength that reminded Igon of his dear old mum. Poor Igon, no matter what he did, it always seemed to be wrong.

'No-one likes me,' he thought, as the good Doctor bashed his head against the iron door and slightly dented it – not the door, his head. 'The only person speaks kindly to me and likes me at all is Valentine.'

The knocking of Igon's head on the door was heard in the Vampires' rooms five minutes' walk away. A Got servant was sent hurrying to answer the door before it was knocked down.

The servant opened the door to a strange scene. There stood two grown men and the taller one seemed to be using the smaller one as a door knocker. The servant had only started to work at the castle that week and had come to the conclusion that the things that went on around the castle were, to say the least, a little strange.

Only on his second day he saw something that would live with him for ever; maybe even longer. He

8

had seen in the castle grounds a 'Cowraffe'. He later found out that a Cowraffe was a cow that had been crossed with a giraffe so that you could milk it from a standing position.

The Doctor looked at the servant, and gave him a slightly embarrassed grin. 'I'm Doctor Plump.'

The servant said, 'Oh, I know you. You're the doctor that looked after my old uncle when he was terribly ill.'

'Oh, did I really? Yes, well ... er, how is he now?' asked the Doctor proudly.

'Dead.'

'Dead?' said the Doctor, a little less proudly.

'Yes.'

'How long?'

'Five foot ten.'

'I mean how long has he been dead?' The Doctor was getting to the knuckle-cracking stage again. He went on. 'What did he die of?'

'Too much weight.'

'Over-indulgence?' the Doctor asked.

'No, over in Germany,' came the reply. 'Won't you come in?'

'Thank you,' the Doctor said, glad to change the subject.

'I suppose you are expected?'

'Yes I am,' the skinny Doctor smiled; well, almost smiled.

'What about ... er ... that?' The servant pointed to Igon.

The Doctor looked down at what he had just used as a door knocker and kicked him hard on the rump. 'If I had my way I'd feed him to the wolves.' And with that he walked past the servant.

The servant bent down and looked Igon straight in the eye.

'Clear off you terrible-looking thing.'

'I want to come in. I want to see Valentine,' Igon said.

'I'm not at all sure that you are allowed in here.'

'Of course I'm allowed in. Why, I'm almost one of the family,' the moving bundle of rags said. He then pushed his way past the servant and ran after the fast retreating Doctor.

The three of them ran along the corridors of the castle towards the Vampires' rooms. They came to a halt outside a door with the letters VIP on it.

'This is it,' cried Igon. 'This is the room. Yes. See VIP. It means Vampire In Pain.'

'Are you sure?' asked the Doctor.

'Of course I'm sure.' Igon jumped up and down with excitement and the thought that today he would see Valentine who liked him and never called him ugly or kicked him.

The Doctor turned to the servant and asked him if it was the correct room.

'I don't really know. I've only worked here for a week and I've never seen Mr Valentine.'

'*Prince* Valentine,' Igon corrected.

'Prince, if you like. But either way I don't know where he is. But he could be in here because VIP means Very Important Person and Mr ... sorry ... Prince Valentine is just that.'

The Doctor nodded his head wisely.

Igon opened the door and walked slowly into the room, followed by the not-too-sure Doctor and the servant.

The room was bereft of all furniture except for a

thick, long wooden table on which rested a coffin with the lid open. From inside the coffin they heard a cough.

Igon whispered, 'There's someone coughing in the coffin.'

The servant kicked Igon, thinking that it was his turn to kick him. The three of them walked tentatively over to the coffin and looked inside; well, the Doctor and the servant did. Poor Igon couldn't reach. So he started to climb up the side of Doctor Plump like a mountain climber making his way up the Matterhorn.

When he saw inside the coffin he was very sad for there was Valentine and it seemed pretty obvious that he was a very sick Vampire.

In the Doctor's mind there was no doubt that Valentine had the vapours. As everyone knows, a Vampire with the vapours is almost as bad as Frankenstein's monster with a screw loose; his head falls off.

Now, when a Vampire has the vapours his head doesn't fall off but his teeth drop out. Can you imagine a Vampire without any teeth? He can't bite you. The worst thing he can do is give a good suck.

Igon looked at the Doctor with fear in his eye. The Doctor looked worried while the servant looked forward to leaving. Suddenly the window crashed open and through it came Valentine's father, King Victor the First, Emperor of all Vampires.

He was over six feet tall and was dressed in full Vampire regalia – a most beautiful hand-made evening dress suit, white tie (of course) with an elegant deep, red-lined cloak. All his clothes were obviously made to measure. His hair over his forehead came to

a perfect point just above the bridge of his long, thin, aristocratic nose that flared as he breathed.

Here was the perfect Vampire, the epitome of what everyone thought a Vampire should be. The one that all other Vampires since modelled themselves on. He stood there, an erect, handsome man, as pale as death itself.

'Gutt evenink,' he hissed. The bat on his shoulder settled down to sleep. The three men stood to attention, well, two of them did. Igon did his best.

'Did my Vamp have a nice evening out?' Igon asked, much to the surprise of both the Doctor and the servant.

'Yes, mine ugly frent,' Victor the First whispered hoarsely. He then glided over to his son lying in the coffin.

'Is vot is in your mind, mine Herr, the same as vot is in mine mind, mine Doctor?'

The Doctor looked away.

'Do you think the same think as I am thinking? I think that mine son has got the dreaded and vile Vampire vapours.'

The Doctor could only nod his long face. King Victor's eyes almost burnt through the shaking Doctor Plump.

'Then I look very much forward to you curink him, mine Doctor.'

The Doctor almost had the vapours himself as he heard what the King said.

'But your Vampship ... er ... no one has ever cured a Vampire of the vapours ... ever.'

'Then you vill be the first, Doctor.'

'But ... Bu ... t.'

Igon, whose head only came up to the Doctor's

13

knees, watched his knees start to shake, rattle and roll. Victor the First carried on talking.

'Mine dear Doctor. If you do not cure mine youn-kest son, the baby of mine family, if you do not cure him ... then I'm afraid you vill cure no von else, ever again. I repeat, if you do not cure him ant restore him back to normal health, then I'm afraid I shall have to giff you to Vernon to experiment vit. That means, Doctor Plump, that you vill probably leef this castle in a bucket. Vernon has a liking for that sort of think. A small bucket; the type children use at the seaside. Ant I promise you, Doctor Plump, although the bucket may be small, all off you vill be in it.'

The bat fell off Victor's shoulders in a deep sleep. Victor caught it in the toe of his Italian, hand-made

The Reluctant Vampire

ERIC MORECAMBE

It is a wild, stormy night in the small village of Katchem-by-the-Throat, in the tiny country of Gotcha, where the unhappy Gots are still ruled by Vampires after four hundred years. At Bloodstock Castle lives Victor, King of the Vampires, and his devoted wife, Queen Valeeta. They have two sons: Vernon, who has a nasty habit of turning people into stone, and Valentine, who reveals the horrible fact that he can't stand the taste of blood! That's only the beginning of an incredible story that will keep readers of all ages in stitches!

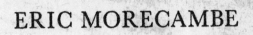

ERIC MORECAMBE

The
Reluctant Vampire

Illustrated by Tony Ross

MAMMOTH

This book is dedicated to

Steven James Bartholomew
Julian Gibbs
Ian Cockhill
Kingsley Roberts
Tom Barnes
and Darcey Cohill

Their knowledge of Vampires and their habits was
invaluable.

First published in Great Britain 1982
by Methuen Children's Books Ltd
Magnet edition published 1983
Reprinted 1984, 1985, 1986 and 1987
Published 1990 by Mammoth
an imprint of Mandarin Paperbacks
Michelin House, 81 Fulham Road, London SW3 6RB

Mandarin is an imprint of the Octopus Publishing Group

ISBN 0 7497 0315 6

A CIP catalogue record for this title
is available from the British Library

Reproduced, printed and bound in Great Britain by
BPCC Hazell Books
Aylesbury, Bucks, England
Member of BPCC Ltd.

Contents

CHAPTER 1

Valentine arises,
As Dr Plump advises.

It was January in the year of seventeen ninety-nine.
The sky was as wet and as black as a bottle of ink. A
shaft of blue lightning suddenly lit up the seven-
hundred-year-old castle on top of a hill. Small yellow
lights flickered from behind a barred window in the
highest room of the highest turret. For a few seconds
before the lightning went out, the castle was silhouetted against thick, huge clouds, fat with rain. The wind
bent double the tallest trees on the hill. They almost
creaked with pain. The moon could occasionally be
seen flying through the clouds at what seemed an
incredible speed. Suddenly, it threw a few seconds of
yellow light on to a thin ribbon of road leading up to
the drawbridge of the silent castle.

On the road was a small coach being pulled by a

very frightened horse. The driver was Doctor Plump. Although his name was Plump, he was the thinnest man you could ever imagine. He was six feet six inches tall but when he wore his top hat he was seven feet six inches tall, and when he was on horseback he was well over ten feet tall.

Doctor Plump was a humourless man with lips as thin as a grasshopper's legs. A large Roman nose – almost large enough for a Roman to sit on – hung between his small, piggy eyes. His eyes were so deep set in his head they looked as if they had been put there with a Black and Decker.

He had been summoned to the castle urgently. His poor horse was wet through with rain and perspiration. The fear showed in its eyes as they rolled round faster than an old woman's birthday. Doctor Plump urged the animal forward with the snap of a long whip that stung the horse like an injection from a blunt syringe, and they sped towards their goal, Bloodstock Castle, overlooking the small village of Katchem-by-the-Throat in the tiny mid-European country of Gotcha.

The 'Gots' were an unhappy people with no king of their own or even a president to rule them. They were ruled by the Vampires of Bloodstock Castle and had been for the past four hundred years.

The horse clattered over the wooden drawbridge as it took the carriage and Doctor Plump inside the courtyard. The Doctor pulled the horse to a halt, jumped off the coach and with his black doctor's bag in his hand, ran towards the massive iron and wooden door, leaving the tired, bewildered horse covered in a cloud of hot steam.

He pulled hard on an iron bar with a handle

attached. A bell sounded inside the castle loud enough to awaken the dead and their friends, the undead, who are like their dead friends but can come back to life again.

Dr Plump waited, wrapping his long, black scarf closer around his thin, scrawny neck. The echo of the bell died down and then the only sound was the rain hitting his top hat as loud as the chattering teeth of an Eskimo with flu.

From inside, the Doctor heard bars being drawn to allow the great door to be opened. It opened, but no more than a crack. He looked into the one black eye of Igon.

Igon was as ugly as it was possible to be. In fact, uglier. He had only one eye, hence the name Igon. A glass eye hung round his neck in a pouch but he only used it on certain occasions such as reading the paper. He would sometimes put it in his trouser pocket to see how much money he had left.

The Doctor spoke.

'Doctor Plump,' he wheezed.

'No, I'm not. I'm Igon,' said Igon and slammed the door.

The Doctor was left in the pouring rain, the driving wind and the dark night. He thumped as hard as he could on the great iron door.

'Igon!' he shouted against the door and the wind.

'Who is it?' said a voice from the other side of the door.

'Doctor Plump,' the wet doctor shouted.

'He's not here,' Igon shouted back.

'No. *I'm* Plump.'

'You should go on a diet then,' said Igon, who wasn't the cleverest person in the world.

3

'Please, I'm Doctor Plump.' He put his mouth closer to the door. 'I've been summoned.'

After a second or two the iron bars were once again removed from their sockets and the door creaked open a little. The same, single, black eye peered out.

The Doctor spoke very quickly. 'I'm Doctor Plump and His Most Gracious Vampari, King Victor, sent for me to have a look at His Serene Vampary Prince Valentine.'

The door opened slowly. 'Come in,' Igon said gruffly.

The Doctor walked in with one long stride. Igon shut the door. Doctor Plump looked around the large hall. It was very dimly lit with no fire to help dry his wet clothes or furniture on which to lay his top hat and overcoat; it was just a very large, very high, freezing cold castle.

The Doctor looked down at Igon. He saw a small, twisted body with a hideous face. His back was bent double with the weight of a large hump that made him walk with his left shoulder nearer to the ground than his right one. His clothes (if you could call them that) were rags. Igon looked up as the Doctor looked down. Igon smiled, showing a most beautiful set of gums.

'Follow me.' He slid along the floor away from the door. 'This way, please, Doctor Pump.'

'Plump,' the Doctor checked. 'Doctor Plump.'

'That's what I said, Pump. I have great difficulty saying my 'l's as I have no teeth, so saying difficulty was even more difficult for me than saying Plump, Doctor Pump.' Igon shuffled towards some distant steps.

The Doctor, a little nonplussed, followed behind him. He tried to make a little light conversation.

4

'It's a wild night.'

'What do you expect for July?'

'But it's January,' the Doctor said in a small, surprised voice.

'I'll bet it gets worse in August,' Igon snarled. The Doctor looked mystified.

They had by now reached the steps, which spiralled round a huge wall like a vine round a tree. The steps were no more than eighteen inches wide, with no handrail. One side of the steps clung to the wall, on the other side was an empty space. One slip and you could fall to the stone flags below and be given a rather large collection of broken ribs. The safest way to climb them was slowly and carefully and to keep one open-palmed hand almost glued to the wall for support. The Doctor nervously followed Igon.

Igon's bent body found great difficulty in climbing the steps, taking at least half a minute to move from one to the next. The Doctor, following Igon, looked up at all the steps they still had to climb and worked out quickly in his mind that at the rate Igon was climbing they would both be forty-five minutes older by the time they reached the top.

'Do you think that maybe I should go first?' the Doctor asked courteously, trying not to offend the bent, broken body in front of him.

'No,' came the painfully grunted reply. 'We'll rest for a while.'

'Rest?' the Doctor questioned. 'Rest?' Good Lord, we've only walked up five steps.'

'You may have only walked up five steps but, my long thin friend, I've climbed them. We shall rest.'

Igon sat on the sixth step trying to get his breath. The Doctor stood towering over him and watched.

After two minutes of gasping and heavy bronchial breathing, Igon slowly took his glass eye out, spat on it and quickly rubbed it with one of the rags he was wearing. He held it in front of him between his thumb and first finger and said, 'It gets darker as we go higher.'

Eventually, they reached the top of the stairs and on the landing they saw the door leading into the unliving quarters of the Vampire King and Queen, Prince Valentine and Valentine's brother, Prince Vernon.

Vernon was mean and hateful. He was the least liked in the family. He was also the elder of the two brothers.

The Doctor waited for Igon to knock on the door. As this didn't happen, he said slowly and with a touch of annoyance:

'Are you going to knock or have you got a key?'

'It's no good knocking. The rooms where they reside are at least another five minutes' walk along the corridors.'

'I see,' the Doctor said with a forced calm. 'So I presume that you have a key to get us past this massive door?' He gave Igon a stiff grin.

'Of course,' said Igon nervously.

'Well?' the Doctor asked.

'Yes I am, thank you. I'm very well, considering,' Igon smiled once more to the Doctor.

'Pardon?' questioned the Doctor, trying to work out the conversation.

'What?' said Igon, not letting his eye look straight at the Doctor's.

'What do you mean, what?' asked the Doctor, who in spite of the cold was beginning to lose his cool.

'What do you mean, what do you mean? Eh? What?' Igon was playing for time. The Doctor started to twitch, first his eye, then his bottom lip. He was getting almost to the exasperated stage. Self-control was more difficult to find. His temper was starting to show. You could always tell when his temper was ready to get the better of him. It was then that he started to crack his knuckles. Unfortunately, he was cracking them on Igon's head.

'The key. Where's the key, you curled up lout?' he whispered viciously.

'On the table,' Igon replied in a hurt voice.

'Which table?' the Doctor asked with controlled hysteria.

Igon pulled himself up to an almost upright position and with his gnarled hand pointed down the steps, and, with a dignity that any monarch would be proud of, said, 'On the table, sir. The one in the kitchen.'

The matchstick-thin Doctor suddenly burst into tears; uncontrollable, fast-flowing tears that ran from his eyes like two small rivers in flood and about to burst their banks.

Igon was fascinated. He had never seen two eyes cry before. He had only ever seen one eye cry and that was his own when his mother used to hit him for being ugly, which was every day. Then he would look in the mirror at his one crying eye. He cried because he was so very ugly, not because of the pain inflicted by his mother's heavy hand.

He would look in that mirror and wonder why he was so very ugly and ask his reflection 'Why am I so ugly?' . . . 'No one is ever going to love me. No one is ever going to want me as their friend. I'm going to go through life always being lonely. I'm so ugly even *I* wouldn't want to be friends with me.' And he would watch a tear roll down from his eye.

Then, taking his glass eye out of his pocket, he would look at it and wonder why it didn't cry. After all, it was an eye; his eye. But poor Igon was never told it wasn't an eye at all. It was only a blue glass marble that had been in a Christmas cracker which he'd stolen and pulled. He pulled it alone as no-one wanted to share a cracker, let alone Christmas, with him and, of course, he was fascinated when the eye (as he thought) dropped out. As far as Igon was concerned, it was Heaven's work.

By now the half-crazed Doctor had grabbed Igon and was shaking him with a fierceness and strength that reminded Igon of his dear old mum. Poor Igon, no matter what he did, it always seemed to be wrong.

'No-one likes me,' he thought, as the good Doctor bashed his head against the iron door and slightly dented it – not the door, his head. 'The only person speaks kindly to me and likes me at all is Valentine.'

The knocking of Igon's head on the door was heard in the Vampires' rooms five minutes' walk away. A Got servant was sent hurrying to answer the door before it was knocked down.

The servant opened the door to a strange scene. There stood two grown men and the taller one seemed to be using the smaller one as a door knocker. The servant had only started to work at the castle that week and had come to the conclusion that the things that went on around the castle were, to say the least, a little strange.

Only on his second day he saw something that would live with him for ever; maybe even longer. He had seen in the castle grounds a 'Cowraffe'. He later found out that a Cowraffe was a cow that had been crossed with a giraffe so that you could milk it from a standing position.

The Doctor looked at the servant, and gave him a slightly embarrassed grin. 'I'm Doctor Plump.'

The servant said, 'Oh, I know you. You're the doctor that looked after my old uncle when he was terribly ill.'

'Oh, did I really? Yes, well ... er, how is he now?' asked the Doctor proudly.

'Dead.'

'Dead?' said the Doctor, a little less proudly.

'Yes.'

'How long?'

'Five foot ten.'

'I mean how long has he been dead?' The Doctor was getting to the knuckle-cracking stage again. He went on. 'What did he die of?'

'Too much weight.'

'Over-indulgence?' the Doctor asked.

'No, over in Germany,' came the reply. 'Won't you come in?'

'Thank you,' the Doctor said, glad to change the subject.

'I suppose you are expected?'

'Yes I am,' the skinny Doctor smiled; well, almost smiled.

'What about ... er ... that?' The servant pointed to Igon.

The Doctor looked down at what he had just used as a door knocker and kicked him hard on the rump. 'If I had my way I'd feed him to the wolves.' And with that he walked past the servant.

The servant bent down and looked Igon straight in the eye.

'Clear off you terrible-looking thing.'

'I want to come in. I want to see Valentine,' Igon said.

'I'm not at all sure that you are allowed in here.'

'Of course I'm allowed in. Why, I'm almost one of the family,' the moving bundle of rags said. He then pushed his way past the servant and ran after the fast retreating Doctor.

The three of them ran along the corridors of the castle towards the Vampires' rooms. They came to a halt outside a door with the letters VIP on it.

'This is it,' cried Igon. 'This is the room. Yes. See VIP. It means Vampire In Pain.'

'Are you sure?' asked the Doctor.

'Of course I'm sure.' Igon jumped up and down with excitement and the thought that today he would see Valentine who liked him and never called him ugly or kicked him.

The Doctor turned to the servant and asked him if it was the correct room.

'I don't really know. I've only worked here for a week and I've never seen Mr Valentine.'

'*Prince* Valentine,' Igon corrected.

'Prince, if you like. But either way I don't know where he is. But he could be in here because VIP means Very Important Person and Mr ... sorry ... Prince Valentine is just that.'

The Doctor nodded his head wisely.

Igon opened the door and walked slowly into the room, followed by the not-too-sure Doctor and the servant.

The room was bereft of all furniture except for a

thick, long wooden table on which rested a coffin with the lid open. From inside the coffin they heard a cough.

Igon whispered, 'There's someone coughing in the coffin.'

The servant kicked Igon, thinking that it was his turn to kick him. The three of them walked tentatively over to the coffin and looked inside; well, the Doctor and the servant did. Poor Igon couldn't reach. So he started to climb up the side of Doctor Plump like a mountain climber making his way up the Matterhorn.

When he saw inside the coffin he was very sad for there was Valentine and it seemed pretty obvious that he was a very sick Vampire.

In the Doctor's mind there was no doubt that Valentine had the vapours. As everyone knows, a Vampire with the vapours is almost as bad as Frankenstein's monster with a screw loose; his head falls off.

Now, when a Vampire has the vapours his head doesn't fall off but his teeth drop out. Can you imagine a Vampire without any teeth? He can't bite you. The worst thing he can do is give a good suck.

Igon looked at the Doctor with fear in his eye. The Doctor looked worried while the servant looked forward to leaving. Suddenly the window crashed open and through it came Valentine's father, King Victor the First, Emperor of all Vampires.

He was over six feet tall and was dressed in full Vampire regalia – a most beautiful hand-made evening dress suit, white tie (of course) with an elegant deep, red-lined cloak. All his clothes were obviously made to measure. His hair over his forehead came to

a perfect point just above the bridge of his long, thin, aristocratic nose that flared as he breathed.

Here was the perfect Vampire, the epitome of what everyone thought a Vampire should be. The one that all other Vampires since modelled themselves on. He stood there, an erect, handsome man, as pale as death itself.

'Gutt evenink,' he hissed. The bat on his shoulder settled down to sleep. The three men stood to attention, well, two of them did. Igon did his best.

'Did my Vamp have a nice evening out?' Igon asked, much to the surprise of both the Doctor and the servant.

'Yes, mine ugly frent,' Victor the First whispered hoarsely. He then glided over to his son lying in the coffin.

'Is vot is in your mind, mine Herr, the same as vot is in mine mind, mine Doctor?'

The Doctor looked away.

'Do you think the same think as I am thinking? I think that mine son has got the dreaded and vile Vampire vapours.'

The Doctor could only nod his long face. King Victor's eyes almost burnt through the shaking Doctor Plump.

'Then I look very much forward to you curink him, mine Doctor.'

The Doctor almost had the vapours himself as he heard what the King said.

'But your Vampship ... er ... no one has ever cured a Vampire of the vapours ... ever.'

'Then you vill be the first, Doctor.'

'But ... Bu ... t.'

Igon, whose head only came up to the Doctor's

knees, watched his knees start to shake, rattle and
roll. Victor the First carried on talking.

'Mine dear Doctor. If you do not cure mine youn-
kest son, the baby of mine family, if you do not cure
him ... then I'm afraid you vill cure no von else, ever
again. I repeat, if you do not cure him ant restore him
back to normal health, then I'm afraid I shall have to
giff you to Vernon to experiment vit. That means,
Doctor Plump, that you vill probably leef this castle
in a bucket. Vernon has a liking for that sort of think.
A small bucket; the type children use at the seaside.
Ant I promise you, Doctor Plump, although the
bucket may be small, all off you vill be in it.'

The bat fell off Victor's shoulders in a deep sleep.
Victor caught it in the toe of his Italian, hand-made

14

shoes just before it hit the ground. He continued as if nothing had happened.

'Do you remember Mayor Goop off Katchem?'

The white-faced Doctor nodded.

'Did you ever vonder vot became off him?'

Once again the Doctor nodded and gulped.

'Vell, vould you like to take him off mine shoe ant put him on mine shoulder?'

At this point the servant fainted on top of the already-fainted Doctor Plump.

Victor the First looked at both of them lying at his feet. He stepped over them with great poise, and placed his hand on the forehead of his still son. With closed eyes he stood for a few seconds. Within that time ice began to form around the inside of the coffin.

'Ve must keep him cold, Igon, mine ugly frent.' He then patted Igon on his head, leaving a snowball resting there. He walked over to the open window, stood on the edge and looked down at the village four hundred feet below. Flicking the ex-Mayor awake with his fingers he looked once more at his son, and said to Igon:

'If mine vife should come lookink for me, tell her I've gone to the blood bank in the village to make a withdrawal, ya?' and with that he jumped.

Igon ran to the window and waved into the darkness. He closed the window with difficulty, thinking 'It's all very well for these people to leave by windows, but I wish they'd close them.' He looked back into the room.

The Doctor and the servant were starting to stir. Both of them stood up rather shakily at first, trying to work out what had happened.

15

When the Doctor at last fully realised the terrible situation he was in, he burst into tears and lay down on the floor, kicking his legs in the air like a badly brought-up child who has been given too much of its own way.

'Help me. Please help me!' he shouted. 'I don't want to leave here in a bucket. Igon, you are my friend. 'Can't you think of anything to save me?'

'Why should I? Earlier you called me a curled up lout.'

'You're not. I'll give you money. I'm not a rich man but I'll give you all the money I have if you will only help me. Please, Igon. Please help me, my friend.'

'How much is all your money?' Igon asked.

'I'll give you fifty krooms,' sobbed the Doctor.

'Sixty.'

'But I haven't got sixty. I've only got fifty.'

'It's not enough,' Igon said stubbornly.

'But can't you get it through that thick skull of yours, you bent idiot, it's all I've got.'

'Now it's gone up to sixty-five krooms for calling me a bent idiot. I'll let you off for saying I have a thick skull.'

'All right, all right,' the Doctor said, knowing he wasn't going to get much change out of Igon. 'Sixty-five krooms.'

'O.K. Shake.'

'I am shaking.'

'No, I mean shake hands.'

They shook hands.

'You heard that, didn't you?' Igon said to the servant. 'You heard him say he'd give me sixty-five krooms.'

The servant who was still in a state of shock nodded vaguely.

Igon shouted to the Doctor, 'He heard you. He heard you. The servant heard you.'

'Yes, yes,' shouted the agitated Doctor, 'but how can you help me?'

'Easy,' answered Igon.

For the first time that evening the Doctor smiled a real, genuine smile. Igon carried on.

'Now, it's obvious that you do not want to leave this place in a small bucket, right?'

'Right,' said the smiling Doctor, eagerly.

'Right,' repeated Igon, 'So – and this is the clever part – I'll hide the bucket.' He flashed his gums and continued. 'Now give me sixty-five krooms.'

The Doctor looked at him with a frozen smile on his face for at least a minute, a thousand things chasing through his head. But one thought kept leaping up in front of the others. It kept asking, 'Is he joking or does he mean that last stupid remark?'

Within the next few seconds the Doctor realised that Igon meant it. He could tell by the vacant look in his eye. Their three eyes held each other till the spell was broken by the Doctor who whispered in a soft voice, convulsed with fear;

'You stupid, twisted fool. Hiding the bucket is no good.' His voice became louder. 'You can't just hide the bucket, you ... you ...' He was at a loss for words.

'You owe me sixty-five krooms,' Igon said defiantly.

'Shut up you stupid, knotted nit,' the Doctor shouted back at him, going quite red in his face.

'I'm not a knotted nit,' said Igon sadly.

17

The servant by now was leaning over the coffin, busily sucking a piece of ice.

'Valentine's moving,' he said, wiping his chin. The Doctor and Igon raced to the coffin. The now near-hysterical Doctor grabbed the lapels of Valentine's evening dress suit and started to shake him.

'Wake up, sir. Please wake up, sir,' the Doctor begged.

Valentine opened his eyes.

'Hello,' he said quietly, his head resting in the crook of the Doctor's arm.

They all looked down at him. He was a most hand-some young man, not a bit like a Vampire; more like a normal person.

'I'm very hungry,' he said.

'Me too. Me too.'

Igon received a blow on the head that was so quick he didn't know whether the Doctor or the servant had done it.

'I really am hungry.' Valentine slowly sat up.

The Doctor grabbed Igon by the hair and pulled a few rags from his throat and offered the exposed throat to Valentine, saying, 'Here, Sir, try this until we can get you something better.'

'No thank you,' said Valentine nicely, much to the relief of Igon.

'I'll shake Igon for you, Sir. You're not supposed to take medicine without it being shaken.'

The Doctor shook Igon so vigorously that a cloud of dust came from his old clothes. He once again exposed Igon's neck towards Valentine.

'No thank you. I don't like blood.'

For a few seconds everyone was still.

'Pardon?'

'I don't like blood, so would you mind putting Igon
away please.' Valentine asked. The Doctor dropped
Igon hard on the floor.

'You don't drink blood?' he said incredulously.

'No. To be quite honest with you, it makes me feel
a bit queasy.'

'How long, Sir, may I ask, have you not been
drinking blood?'

'You may not believe this, but all my life. As a
matter of fact, I don't like any of the food we Vampires are supposed to eat or drink. I like chips and I
like a small glass of red wine.

For years I've been kidding everybody I've been
drinking blood, but I change it for red wine. Father
doesn't know – or Vernon either. I have a feeling that
Mother knows, but I'm not positive. I don't know
why I'm telling you all this. I don't even know who
you are, or worse, if I can trust you. Of course, I know
I can trust Igon because I look upon him as a friend.'

The servant and the Doctor looked at Igon who was now smiling gummily at everyone. The Doctor was the first to speak.

'Of course he's your friend, sir. He's our friend too,' he said, patting Igon on his head. 'Maybe we should introduce ourselves. I'm Doctor Plump.'

Valentine's hand came out of the coffin to be shaken by the Doctor. The servant walked slowly over to the coffin and said:

'My name is Sed.'

'Is that your first name?' asked Valentine.

'No Sir. Sed's my last name.'

'Well, tell his Vampship your first name then,' Doctor Plump snarled.

'My first name is a traditional Gotcha name, Sir. It's Ronnoco.'

'Yes, that's a traditional Gotcha name all right,' Igon said, not wanting to be left out of the conversation.

'So,' said Valentine. 'Your name is Ronnoco Sed?'

'Yes Sir,' The servant nodded.

'How long have you been working here, Ronnoco?'

'I started last week, Sir.'

'And may I ask what you did before you came here?'

'I was a troubadour, Sir. I used to sing. I toured our country and sang to the people of the cities and the villages.'

'And why are you now working here as a servant?' Valentine inquired nicely.

'The people of the cities and the villages didn't want me to sing to them.'

'Sir, would you mind lying down in your coffin,' pleaded Dr Plump. 'After all, I am the doctor and you do have the vile Vampire vapours so you need all the rest you can get.'

'I'm getting up,' Valentine told them. 'I'm getting up if someone will give me a hand.'

'But you can't . . .' the Doctor spluttered, thinking of leaving the castle in a small bucket.

'I haven't got the vapours. The only thing I have at the moment is a chill from staying out late the other night.'

The relief on the Doctor's face was a sight to behold.

The Doctor helped Valentine down from the coffin to the floor. The four of them quietly left the room, Valentine with the specific intention of telling his mother not to worry. He was feeling better.

CHAPTER 2

King Victor smiles with venomous grace
At Wilf the Werewolf's hairy face.

In the village of Katchem the clock had just struck midnight, although the hands said the time was a quarter to twelve. The reason was that Victor was sitting on the pointer, his cloak billowing in the wind.

Above the din of the clock and the strong wind, the four people in the tavern heard the howling of a lone wolf; a long, piercing sound that almost stopped the blood flowing through the body. A howl so chilling as to make the serving girl, Areta, drop and break an empty Stein mug she was clearing off a table. Her father, Klaus Grabbo, who owned the tavern, gave her a look of annoyance. She, in return, gave him a quick look of apology.

Then the wolf stopped howling and within seconds

the large window next to the door burst open and Victor stood in its frame. A flash of lightning lit up the tavern for a mere second, followed by a deathly silence. Areta and her father, with their two customers, stood like statues.

'Gutt evenink,' Victor the First said, smiling, showing a fine set of teeth of which two were noticeably longer than the others. 'I vould like a drink, mine host. A drink out of mine special bottle, ya?'

He crossed to the bar with the movement, ease and grace of mercury on glass. Grabbo picked out a bottle hidden at the back of the bar.

The liquid in the bottle was blood red. With a shaking hand Grabbo poured from the bottle until Victor hissed, 'Enough'. Then, with a hard look

around the room at the other two customers, he raised
the glass to his lips with the Vampires' toast:

> A soldier's in love with his rifle,
> A sailor's in love with his deck,
> A Vampire's in love when he kisses a girl
> And leaves two holes in her neck

He swallowed the blood red liquid in one fast gulp.
The other two customers kept their eyes averted from
Victor, not wanting to antagonise him in any way
and not wanting to be noticed by him either. Victor
smacked his lips and said:

'Excellent. Really very gutt. Eighteen years olt,
I vould say, ya?'

The landlord picked up the bottle and looked at it
before answering. 'Nineteen,' he said.

'Nineteen? Vos she really? I vould haff said eighteen. Maybe, mine bar-keeping frent, you are keeping
it too cool. I don't like it ven it's too cool. Unterstant,
Grabbo? I don't like it ven it's too colt, ya?'

'Yes, Sir.' Grabbo grovelled. Areta continued to
clear the tables although she had done them twice
already.

Victor watched her, a smile coming to his lips. 'You
know somethink, Grabbo?'

'Sir?'

'You daughter has become very beautiful, ya?'

'Er ... thank you, Sire.'

'Ya, very beautiful inteed. Giff me a drink off the
twenty year olt.'

Grabbo filled the waiting glass from another hidden bottle.

'Vill you join me, mine frent?'

'Er no, Your Greatness. Er ... I'm off it at the

24

moment. I'm ... er ... trying to lose weight,' Grabbo quickly lied, not wanting to offend a customer.

'I haff the perfect vay off losing veight. Vot you do is simple – like your two customers over there.' Victor looked very hard at the two other customers. 'You eat nothing but roobs, ant then ...'

'Roobs?' questioned Grabbo.

'Yah, roobs.'

'What are roobs, Sir?'

'Roobs are a special fruit. They are very rare ant are only to be fount ten feet unterground.'

'But, how will they help me to lose weight, if I may ask, Sire?'

'It's obvious. The exercise vile you are diggink for them. And then, ven you haff fount them you von't eat them because they have such a horrit taste. That vay you vill lose even more veight, ya?' Here Victor burst into almost uncontrollable laughter; laughter so chilling that the mirror behind the bar cracked.

Grabbo looked into the mirror. He could see his own reflection and the look of terror on his own pale face. He could also see the entire room. But he could not see Victor who was stood next to him because, being a Vampire, Victor had no reflection.

'I'm sorry, mine frent,' Victor said, looking at the cracked mirror and although Grabbo couldn't see the reflection of Victor, Victor looked towards the mirror and straightened his tie.

A long scratch at the door of the tavern made everyone, including Victor, turn their heads. No one moved. The door slowly creaked open. There stood a smiling werewolf, a man covered in long, shaggy wolfhair looking a bit dishevelled on account of the rather strong wind. He had the werewolf's almost red,

25

fiery eyes and long, canine teeth. He stood erect in the doorway with the wind blowing his long hair as a woman blows on a fur coat. King Victor looked at him and thought he looked like a rather untidy crow's nest.

'Come in, Vilf, ant close the toor,' Victor said.

Wilf the Werewolf, as he was known, walked into the tavern, shutting the door behind him.

'Hello Victor,' he said in a rather sing-song voice. 'How's the wife and kids?' He was pleased to be indoors on such a night as this and he showed it by wagging his tail.

'They are all very vell, thank you, mine covered-in-hair frent, and it vos very nice of you to ask.'

'Not at all,' Wilf smiled. 'You know me. I'm very fond of your brood. How's poor Valentine? Is he any better?'

'Whom tolt you he vos ill?'

'Dick.'

'Tick?'

'Yes, Dick. You remember Dick ... Dick the big, daft dwarf,' he almost barked.

26

'Ah yes, Tick. Tick the bick taft twarf. Ya, I re-member him. Ya.'

'He told me Val wasn't too good,' Wilf continued. 'I met him in the forest and we went for a walkies. That's when he told me.'

'Vell, Valentine's a lot better I think. The Doctor's vith him now. Doctor Plump.'

'Plump?' Wilf thought a while. 'Doctor Plump?'

'Ya.'

'Yes, I think I used to go about with his alsatian. I'm not sure.'

'Very tall.'

'No. Short, rather fat with a scruffy tail.'

'I mean the Doctor.'

'Oh!' Wilf snarled sweetly.

Areta had joined the other two customers while her father was once more behind the bar. Wilf joined Victor at the bar.

'Can I get you anythink?' King Victor asked Wilf.

'No. No thank you, Victor. I'm off it at the moment. The hard stuff, that is. The vet says it's best if I keep off it for a few more days. I've got a touch of hard pad.' He showed Victor the sole of his left foot. 'That's why I'm limping a bit.' He put his hind foot gingerly back on the floor.

'I vould think you get the hard pad from all the runnink you do, ya?'

'Never stop. I'm always running,' Wilf said proudly, turning and leaning his back on the bar.

'Ya, you run a lot, Vilf.'

'I'm always running. Well, you see, farmers are always after me for frightening their sheep and en-raged parents and all that, and bears and the like. Bears don't like us much so they chase us a lot.

Parents, farmers, bears … That's why I do a lot of running, you see. I'll tell you what …'

'Vot?'

'If you were to throw a stick now, across this floor to the other side of the room, I'd run after it. It's our nature, you see.'

'Vould you also brink it back?'

'Sometimes, but sometimes I forget.' Wilf looked around the tavern once more. 'Mind you, I don't run so much when I'm not a werewolf. When I'm an ordinary human being I like to sit at home with my legs up. I rest because I know that as soon as the full moon comes up again I go to bed and in about ten or twenty minutes or so I look down at the back of my hands and the hairs are starting to grow.'

'Vot do you do then?' Victor asked with keen interest.

'Well, I get up and go on to the landing and shout through my mum's door, "The hairs are growing Mum, so I'll be off now and I'll see you in about a week or ten days" and she shouts back something like, "All right, love. Be a good boy and bring back a fresh loaf with you" so then I'm off again, running.'

Wilf finished talking and noticed that everybody in the tavern was listening to him. This made him feel quite important.

Victor nodded agreement all through Wilf's conversation. He turned to Grabbo saying, 'I'll haff one for the road, Grabbo. I'll haff half a forty year olt.' Turning back to Wilf he said:

'I mustn't haff anythink too stronk at the moment. I'm meeting the vife later on ant takink her out for a bite.'

'Where?' asked Wilf with enough interest in his

28

voice to make Victor think, 'He vants to come too.'

'Er, vell, it's more off a small family get-together than anythink else. Just the vife, Vernon, me and Valentine, if he's any better. Ve vill propaply go and vait at the bridle path ant see if there is anythink vorth bitink.'

Victor was trying to get away quickly. 'Oh, gutt Lord, is that the time? I tolt the vife I vould pick her up at twelf thirty.'

'Is that the time she falls down?' Wilf asked.

'Pardon me?' said a puzzled Victor.

'You said you would pick her up at twelve thirty, so I was asking you if that was the time she fell down . . . Twelve thirty?'

'Vilf, I haff never unterstood your jokes ant I still don't. Guttbye Vilf,' Victor said, patting Wilf on the head and giving him a tickle under the chin. Wilf showed his approval by licking Victor's ear.

Victor left the tavern the same way as he had arrived – by the window. Areta went to close the window after him, thinking, 'He's just like all men. Never closes anything after him.'

Grabbo started to clean the glasses and whistled a late night tune. The tune was very popular in Gotcha at the moment. It was called 'Show me the way to my cottage and my bed'. He hoped Wilf and the other two customers might take the hint and realise how late it was. But Wilf was in a talking mood that night.

'Nice man, Victor, eh Grabbo?'

'Charming,' Grabbo said, oozing sarcasm that went straight over Wilf's head. Wilf was quiet for a few seconds and then asked:

'I don't suppose you have anybody fresh in the cold cellar have you Grabbo?'

30

'No,' said Grabbo truthfully while putting the forty year old away.

'It's just that I fancy somebody fresh, that's all.'

'You heard what my father said, Wilf,' Areta said, bustling around and clearing the table of the two customers who took the hint and left without saying goodnight to anyone.

'Well, have you got any crisps then?' Wilf asked.

'What flavour?' Grabbo asked with a tired voice.

After a moment's thought Wilf said, 'Human please.'

Grabbo threw him a pack of crisps saying, 'Smokey bacon, take it or leave it.'

'I'll take it,' Wilf said, his lips and teeth tearing open the packet.

'That will be three lukas.'

'What?' Wilf asked, spraying crisps all over the bar.

'That will be three lukas. Are you going deaf, Wilf?'

'I haven't got three lukas. As a matter of fact I haven't got any money at all.'

'No money? No money at all?' Grabbo said, looking at his daughter.

'No. You see, when I'm a werewolf I haven't any pockets so I can't carry any money.'

'All right, Wilf,' Grabbo said in a bored and tired voice. 'You owe me three lukas.'

'Thanks Grabbo.'

'That's O.K. Now take your crisps and go.'

'Yes. Well goodnight then, Grabbo, and goodnight Areta. By the way, Areta, I'm not a werewolf next week so I was wondering if you would come to the fair with me a week on Thursday?'

'Goodnight Wilf,' Areta said softly.

'Goodnight Areta,' Wilf said sadly.

31

CHAPTER 3

A Vampire family on the street;
A Werewolf with only crisps to eat.

Valentine suddenly stopped Igon by putting his hand
out. The Doctor and the servant behind nearly
bumped into them. Since they had left Valentine's
room the four had been walking along seemingly
endless corridors. Now Valentine had spotted the
motif of a bat biting the throat of another bat on a
door. He turned to his new friends and nodded.

Slowly he opened the door and they all looked into
a very large, beautifully furnished room. Even the
coffin in the middle of the room was made from
Japanese walnut and highly polished. The handles of
the coffin were gold, as was a massive candelabra
holding twelve sixteen-inch lighted candles on a
round, exquisitely-made satinwood table.

'Hello, Mum,' Valentine smiled, directing the

other five eyes to the coffin. 'Mum?' he called, 'are you in there?'

Queen Valeeta's head rose slowly out of the opened coffin. She saw Valentine and smiled.

'Darling. My darling boy,' she breathed heavily. 'Give me a hand, there's a good boy. It's time I rose. I have to meet your father. He's taking us out tonight. You, too, Valentine, if you are well enough.'

Valentine helped his mother out of the coffin. She stood on the floor and swayed for a moment, then quickly composed herself. She took three or four deep breaths then looked at Igon, Doctor Plump and the servant. She raised a quizzical eyebrow at Valentine which asked what these people were doing in her room. She was a strikingly beautiful woman and at the moment was striking Igon beautifully over the head with a lighted candle.

'Who are these people?' she hissed.

'They are my friends,' Valentine said. 'Doctor Plump, Ronnoco Sed and Igon, who you have known since being a little girl.'

'I've never been a little girl,' Igon protested. Ronnoco Sed and Doctor Plump both hit him at the same time.

Vernon suddenly joined them in the room. He didn't come in through the door. He didn't come in through the window. He just appeared in the middle of the room behind a flash of bright blue smoke.

They all looked at Vernon, with a surprised look on their faces, including Vernon himself. This was the first time he had done the trick right. He had transported himself from the cellars up into his mother's room.

33

He stood there, in the middle of the room, dazed and slightly on fire, trying to put himself out by patting himself hard and blowing on himself even harder. He was having little success. At the moment he was smouldering like an old bonfire.

Igon was the first to come to his senses. He picked up a pitcher of water and threw it at Vernon but, sadly, he let go of the pitcher too and it landed slap-bang on the back of Vernon's head.

The pitcher broke on impact, covering him with water and therefore putting out the fire. It also put Vernon out, cold. The Doctor fainted on top of an already fainted Ronnoco Sed for the second time that evening.

Valentine could hardly hold back a smile while his mother laughed out loud and applauded. Igon knew he was in for it as soon as Vernon came round, so he tried to climb up the chimney.

Igon was a very lucky warped old man that night for, just as Vernon came to his senses and was just beginning to think of knocking the already minute

senses completely out of Igon, Victor came into the room through the window. In this household Victor was the King. His word was law.

He looked at his family and the Doctor and the servant and then at Igon scrambling about in the fireplace among the ashes.

'Igon,' he hissed. 'Vot are you doink? Are you arrivink or are you goink, ya?'

Vernon suddenly spoke. 'He hit me, father. That stupid, stunted swine hit me. He hit me with a pitcher.' Vernon, his eyes glowing with rage, glared at poor Igon but Victor's satanic eyes slowly turned towards Vernon and Vernon knew he made a bad mistake in interrupting his father. Quickly and sullenly he murmured an apology. The King hissed softly in a voice filled with venom:

'Since ven has it been permissible to interrupt your father?' He hit Vernon with the flat of his hand across the cheek, leaving a blue mark across his white face. 'Ant since ven,' he continued, 'has it been permissible to interrupt the Kink?'

Once again he slapped Vernon across the other cheek, leaving another blue mark that matched the first one. Vernon's eyes, blood-red with anger, looked steadily at his father. Valentine looked at the ground while Valeeta looked at her husband, her eyes filled with pride and love. Doctor Plump and Ronnoco Sed slept soundly on in their faint.

Igon had stopped scrambling in the ashes and was now trying to cover himself with logs.

'Igon, mine little filty frent. Come here,' Victor commanded.

Igon did as he was told and came to Victor, expecting another powerful blow about his head. Victor

36

put his hand out to rest gently on top of Igon's head, saying:

'Igon, you are the most beautiful ugly think I haff ever seen, ant I've seen a few ugly thinks in mine time. But I haff never seen anythink quite as beautifully ugly as you.'

Igon gave Victor the kind of look an obedient dog gives its master. Victor then playfully kicked Igon to the other side of the room and as Igon rolled over and over, the only thing he could hear was a deep-throated laugh coming from the direction of Victor, King of the Vampires. As Igon rolled to a stop, Victor continued to speak.

'Vell, mine beloved family. Tonight ve vill go out together. How gutt it is to see you lookink so vell, Valentine.'

The Doctor stirred.

'Ah, Doctor. I'm glat to see you. I'm thankink you for curink mine son, Valentine, from the vapours. You see, I knew you could do it.'

The Doctor, who was still not quite himself, got shakily to his feet. Valentine spoke before the Doctor could say anything.

'Yes, Father. The Doctor was very good and also very quick. He found out the cause   and the cure too.'

'Vot was the cause?'

'Er . . . too much blood, Father. I've been drinking too much blood,' Valentine lied, looking sideways at the Doctor, hoping he wouldn't be fool enough to say something else.

'Ant the cure?' Victor asked his son.

'Blood oranges.'

'Blood oranges?'

37

'Yes Father. From now on I have only to eat blood oranges. Isn't that correct, Doctor?'

Doctor Plump half smiled and half nodded.

'The Doctor said that blood oranges would be better than real blood if I want to stay cured of the dreaded Vampire vapours, and you know how contagious they are, Father.'

'Blood oranges are contagious?' asked his Father.

'No Father, the vapours are contagious,' Valentine corrected.

'I see,' said Victor, almost to himself. 'Vell, iff you haff to haff blood oranges, then blood oranges it vill be.' He looked at his wife, who knowing Valentine's feelings about blood, nodded her head in agreement.

'But I'm tellink you this, mine son. Blood oranges vill eventually rot your teeth. Come everyvon. Ve vill all go into the village to celebrate Valentine's recovery.' He led the way to the window.

Valentine didn't want to go out of the window and neither did the Doctor. Nor would Ronnoco Sed when he came round.

'Er . . . Father.'

'Yes, mine son.'

'Maybe I should take the others out by the front door.'

'Vy?'

'Well, they are not like us. They can't turn into bats and fly out of the window.'

'Throw Igon out of the window. Please let me throw Igon out of the window, Father,' Vernon begged.

'There, there, dear,' his mother said. 'Not tonight. Maybe some other night. Now do as your Father asks.'

Victor fixed his eyes on his wife. 'Asks?' he said loudly. 'Asks,' he said even louder. 'Do as your Father tells him, not asks. I am the Kink ant you all do as I command. All off you. Unterstant?'

Vernon and the King of the Vampires looked at each other. The air in the room crackled with electric hate. Vernon backed down under his father's gaze. Victor, knowing he had beaten his son, gave a smile that could freeze two flames together. He looked around the room, his gaze resting on his other son, Valentine.

'Very vell, you take the others out through the front door.' He looked at the Doctor and the servant. 'I vould take you out that vay mineself, but I'm afraid I don't know vere the front door is.'

With that he gathered his wife and Vernon close to him, put his hand inside his cloak pocket, bringing out the ex-mayor of Katchem, and put him on his shoulder. He led them to the window, saying before they all jumped.

'Ve vill see you in the main street, in the doorvay off Motherscares, ya?'

It took Ronnoco Sed a little while to come round fully. The three of them then made their way to the door. Then Valentine looked round and saw Igon huddled in a corner of the room with tears of sadness welling up in his eye.

'Come on,' Valentine called. 'We can't go without you, can we? You are the only one who knows the way.'

Igon wiped the tears away from his eye with his sleeve and ran after his hero, Valentine.

It took them forty minutes to get to the front door and that was at speed. It took Igon forty seconds to

39

get to the same door. He had found a shortcut. To be perfectly honest, the shortcut found him.

He was leaning against a wooden panel along the corridor, trying to get his breath back, when suddenly the panel opened and he fell straight down, landing on the stone flags below, just outside the front door.

Lady Luck continued to be with him that night and luckily the fall was broken by his legs. He didn't cry out in pain, having been taught from the beatings given to him by his lovely and much-missed Mummy to be impervious to pain. He always used to say she had the best left hook he had ever felt and she could have been the world champion heavyweight boxer if she hadn't been disqualified in the tenth for consistent butting.

Igon lay there, thinking of Mummsy and what the other lads would think of him being there before them. They were quite surprised.

Meanwhile, King Victor, Queen Valeeta and Prince Vernon stood in the doorway of Motherscares, sheltering from the rain. They were huddled toget'.er, trying very hard not to attract the attention of Wilf the Werewolf who was across the street, also sheltering from the rain in the doorway of Boots the Cobbler, whose son was in England learning to be a chemist. Of course, everyone wondered what good that would do him.

Wilf stood there, leaning near the window, loudly eating the last of his smokey bacon crisps. It was two in the morning and the rain was still pouring down. Wilf normally wasn't bothered about rain but tonight he wasn't too happy as it was affecting his hard pad and as most of you realise, there's nothing worse for a werewolf than a wet hard pad.

A lonely, huddled figure walked nervously along the pavement. Wilf squeezed back against the shop doorway, trying to press himself against it so as to be almost invisible.

The lonely figure looked round to see if it was being followed and as it passed the entrance to the shop where Wilf was hiding, a parcel fell on to the ground. The figure stooped down to pick it up at the same time as Wilf sprang out to grab the figure.

Victor, Valeeta and Vernon all watched Wilf sail over the top of the bent figure and land in the middle of the road. In all his years (over two hundred of them) Victor had never seen a werewolf with such a surprised look on his face. Its face had the same look a midget would have who had just been told he had won the long jump in the Olympics.

The huddled figure stood up and looked across the road to see Wilf sprawling in the gutter. Instead of running off while it had the opportunity, it walked towards Wilf and helped him out of the road.

'Are you all right, Wilf?'

'Fine thanks, Mum,' Wilf answered back. 'I didn't know it was you. What are you doing out at this time of night?'

'Well dear, I thought you would be about the village, what with it raining so hard and your corns . . .'

'Hard pad, Mum.'

'Oh yes. Well, like I was saying, I thought you'd be around on account of the rain. I thought you wouldn't be going off into the woods and all that scaring the children stuff . . .'

'And grown-ups as well, Mum.'

'Of course, dear . . . in the pouring rain.' Wilf's mum smiled at her son. 'So I've brought your favourite; a toasted cheese sandwich.'

'Aw Mum. Who ever heard of a werewolf eating a toasted cheese sandwich? I mean to say, Mum. Couldn't you have brought something like a pork chop?'

'A pork chop? Why, Wilf Igrate.' She called him by his full name. 'You don't like pork chops. You always say "I don't like pork chops" and here you are in the middle of Katchem, actually asking for pork chops! Well I never. Wilf, you worry me the way you never know what you want. Lord knows, I've accepted the fact that you're a werewolf, although what your father would say if he ever came back I shudder to think. But I honestly cannot get used to your not knowing what you want.'

42

'I tell you what, Mum,' Wilf said, trying his best to get back into her good books. 'I tell you what.'

'What?' she said sharply.

'Leave the sandwich and I will eat it, I promise. Cross my heart.' He drew a cross on his body.

'That's your liver, you big oaf.'

'Well, you know what I mean, Mum.' He put a paw around her ample body and tried to lick her face. She pushed him away gently, saying:

'Stop that, you big soft thing. I'm going home now so if I don't see you, be a good boy and don't forget when you come home I want a loaf. Fresh, mind you.'

Wilf nodded and gave his Mum another quick lick. She walked back up the street, glad she had made the effort and seen her boy.

All through this mother and son reunion the royal family of Vampires stood stock still and watched them from the doorway of Motherscares. Wilf had no idea they were there, and the Vampires were happy to keep it that way, especially Valeeta who really didn't like Wilf on the rather selfish grounds that he could grow his own fur coat, while she had to beg and pray to her husband to get her one. In all fairness he did so, even though the first time she wore it two dogs chased her up a tree.

Wilf would never have seen them at all if it hadn't been for Ronnoco, Doctor Plump, Valentine and Igon coming noisily down the street and stopping in front of Motherscares.

He limped across the street to them, kicking his rolled-up smokey bacon crisp packet in the style of Gotcha's most famous footballer, Cruft, whom Wilf had a tremendous admiration for. Valeeta spoke in a vicious whisper to Victor.

'Get rid of him.'

Victor looked at his wife in surprise. 'Eh?'

'Get rid of him.'

'Who?'

'Him.' She nodded towards Wilf playing football in the middle of the road.

'Vilf?' he asked.

'Yes, Vilf . . . I mean Wilf.'

'You mean kill him?'

'If you have to.'

'But I can't do that.' He spoke quickly and softly out of the corner of his mouth. He always found this difficult to do on account of the rather large teeth on either side. 'He is von of our biggest tourist attractions. He brinks in thousands of gripples a year. It's through him that ve haff vater runnink out off the taps.'

Wilf kicked the rolled crisp packet towards them with all his might and shouted 'Goal'. The 'ball' hit Vernon in the face. As it bounced off his face it left a small piece of crisp on the end of his nose which Wilf licked off. Vernon stood there and fumed.

'Hello everybody,' Wilf said, offering his paw to be shaken. Valentine spoke first.

'Hello Wilf. The way you're playing you'll soon make the national team.'

'Thanks Val. I thought you had the dreaded vapours.'

'No. Er . . . not now. Doctor Plump cured me.'

'Well done, Doc,' Wilf said, walking over to the Doctor and shaking his wet fur all over him. Ronnoco looked at Wilf and passed out on the shop door entrance. Everyone ignored him.

Queen Valeeta was starting to get a little angry

with all the noise and the confusion. It was a mite too much for her. She asked rather loudly what the time was. No one had a watch with them and the village clock was broken because someone kept sitting on the long hand at a quarter to twelve every night. But Wilf told her not to worry about the time as he could easily find out for her.

He went over the road and under a closed, curtained window he began to howl at the top of his voice. After about a minute of howling, the window opened and a voice shouted down to Wilf:

'What are you doing, Wilf? Don't you know that it's almost two thirty in the morning?' and with that slammed his window.

Wilf thanked him and skipped back across the road to Valeeta to tell her the time was two thirty. She was quite impressed with Wilf's guile.

They all stayed there in the shop doorway until it was almost dawn and then, of course, the Vampire family had to go back to the castle to sleep for the rest of the day.

But Valentine wasn't happy. He wanted to get away from all this Vampire business and to live a normal life with a pretty wife and roses around the door of a cottage and the patter of little children's feet, and not the patter of little rats' feet like at the castle. But, sadly, he thought, 'That can't happen. Not for me. I'm a Vampire and that's it. It's the old saying of Vampires: "Home is where your artery is."' Sadly he pulled down his coffin lid and went to sleep.

Vernon thought of diabolical ways of getting rid of Igon before pulling his coffin lid down for the day. King Victor had a daymare, dreaming of living on blood oranges while Queen Valeeta softly smiled to herself in her dream of Wilf.

Wilf stayed in the doorway of Boots and scratched himself to sleep. Ronnoco was left in the doorway of Motherscares, while Doctor Plump went back to his horse and buggy and fell asleep driving home.

Igon sat in the corner of Valentine's room and thought of his dear, old, kind, generous, heavy-fisted Mother. The wry smile on his face was put there by that same fist!

CHAPTER 4

Valentine's shocked at his own reflection.
Vernon wants Igon for closer inspection.

Valentine jumped up quickly and hit his head on the coffin lid. Igon awoke instantly and slid over to Valentine's coffin.

'What can I do, my Prince?' he asked through the closed lid.

'Open the lid, please, Igon,' came a muffled reply.

'Pardon?' asked Igon.

'Open the lid please, Igon,' Valentine's voice said softly but with urgency.

'I'm sorry Sire, but I can't hear you properly. I'll open the lid so that I can hear you.'

Igon opened the lid but hardly more than a crack.

'Thank you, Igon, but could you just open the lid a little more, please?'

'I mustn't, Sire. It's daylight and it's dangerous for Vampires to be abroad in daylight.'

'Just open the lid. It's too heavy from the inside.'

'No, Sire,' Igon was at a loss. Although not a Vampire himself, he knew all the laws and rules of the Vampires' needs and ways.

'Igon,' Valentine nearly shouted. 'Just for the moment I want you to forget all that rhubarb and list ...'

'You want some rhubarb, Sire? I'll fetch some immediately.'

'No, Igon.' This time Valentine did not shout. 'Don't get any rhubarb.' He spoke very precisely and slowly. 'Look, the only thing I want you to do is to open my bed lid. That's all. Just open my bed lid. Now that's got to be simple, Igon, hasn't it.'

'Oh yes, Sire. But it's daylight and what would your father say if he found out I'd let you out in the daylight? You might die and I definitely would.'

'I won't tell him, Igon. Honest, I won't tell him you let me out,' Valentine pleaded through the crack of light. 'Igon, haven't I always been kind to you?'

Igon nodded at the coffin where the sad voice was coming from.

'And haven't I always been on your side and stuck up for you? Haven't I, Igon?'

Igon blinked as a tear rolled down his left cheek. He also looked at his glass eye to see if that was crying, but it wasn't.

'Yes, Sire, you have been the only one,' he sobbed.

'So trust me, Igon. Trust me. Lift the lid and I promise you that nothing will happen to me and nothing, my little friend, will happen to you. I give you my word.'

That was good enough for Igon. Not because Valentine had given his word, although that in itself was enough, but because he had called Igon his little friend. And he had called him little friend without putting words like 'ugly' or 'stupid' in front of it.

Within a few seconds Valentine was sitting up, shading his eyes against the sunlight that was filtering in through the dark, heavy curtains.

'Open the curtains, Igon.'

'Should I, Sire? I don't want you to die, Sire. You are the only friend I've got. If you die, Sire, I might as well die too.' Here Igon looked as sweet as he could, rather like half a lemon that had been squeezed two weeks ago. Valentine gave a smile of thanks and true affection.

'I promise you, Igon. The daylight will not kill me,' he said, and at the same time sprang to the floor. 'Come, let's get some wonderful hot sunlight into this musty old room.'

Valentine strode boldly over to the curtains and with one swift movement threw them apart. Igon ran around the room like a demented gerbil. The entire room was bathed in hot, bright, beautiful, life-giving sunshine.

Igon covered his eye and face with his hands while Valentine looked down on the village below and watched happily as the heat of the sun warmed his body. For the first time he could remember, he felt not only well but good. He wanted to do someone, somewhere, some good. He wanted to share his happiness with someone. He looked at Igon and, still smiling, said:

'It's all right, Igon. I'm still here. You can look at me. I'm not dead. Look at me.'

49

Igon nervously took his hands away from his face and through a squinted eye looked at Valentine who was fully bathed in sunshine.

'This can't be right, Sire,' Igon said with a shaking voice.

'Ah, but it is, Igon, it is,' said Valentine, taking a huge, deep breath.

Igon sat in the middle of the room on the floor, looking quite lost and befuddled.

'Come, Igon,' Valentine continued. 'Let's go to the village and meet some real people. People who we've never seen before. Maybe even a pretty girl.'

'For me?' Igon asked, his eye brightening up.

'Who knows?' Valentine laughed.

They left the castle, Valentine hoping it was for good. He intended to send the King and Queen a night letter thanking them for all they had done for him, but somehow things don't always work out the way you plan.

The first thing they heard when they got to the village was the gossip that Ronnoco had been put in the only cell of the jail for being found supposedly drunk in the doorway of Motherscares.

To both Valentine and Igon the village seemed packed. They had never seen so many people at once. Valentine was very excited at seeing things that he had never seen before. Things like birds in a cage, all singing; beautiful, bright little things. He had never seen birds at the castle. Only once he remembered seeing a vulture flying over the castle when his old Uncle Vermillion had died. It was said that he had fallen down at night on to a stake that somehow had pierced his heart.

Igon, as a boy, had been taken to the village, but he had almost forgotten the things he'd seen. Today the thing that caught his eye was a monocle which he thought he would save up for, then put in his eye pouch for his glass eye.

The whole day for the two of them was spent looking at everything. Igon soon got over the fact that Valentine was still alive and that the daylight hadn't killed him or even slowed him down for that matter. It seemed to make him stronger although it worried Igon slightly that Valentine's skin was starting to turn a little on the red side.

It was now late afternoon. Both of them were starting to feel a little hungry, particularly Igon who was one of those people who could eat a lot of anything at any time. But they had no money and they both knew that in the outside world money was the most important of things and that humans would kill for it.

They stood looking wistfully into the window of Ari Hovis the baker at the hot bread and the beautiful cakes and scones. It was then that Igon noticed his reflection.

His heart missed a beat, if not two or three, not at his own ugliness but the fact that standing next to him in the reflection of the window was Valentine. A thousand thoughts raced through Igon's tiny mind.

'Vampires have no reflection. Should I tell him? Should I tell his father, the King of all the Vampires, that one of his sons had a reflection? What should I do?' He was so agitated he started to jump up and down, so much so that people stopped to watch him doing his jig in the middle of the main street. This ugly little man with a tall, handsome fellow in full evening dress.

But, the people just thought they were from the circus, always due around this time of the year, and that these two fellows were here to advertise it. No one considered it would be anyone from the castle. Why, the only person to be seen from the castle was the King and he was only ever seen at night and very late at that.

Valentine realised they were being stared at, so, in a nice, gentle way he tried to stop Igon from doing this foolish jig. Igon couldn't be stopped and still carried on with his dance, pointing towards the window. He was so excited he couldn't speak.

Valentine looked in the window, saw their reflection and thought they looked like a circus ringmaster and his performing monkey. It was almost a full minute before Valentine realised why Igon was so excited and kept pointing to the window. For the first time, Valentine saw his reflection!

He raised an arm above his head to see if the other person who looked like him would raise his arm. He did. Valentine then lifted his top hat. So did the other fellow in the window. Igon and Valentine walked to the next shop and looked in their window. Yes, they could still see each other. They ran along the street, looking in all the windows, still seeing themselves. They were now shouting with joy, pointing to themselves in the window and to passers-by, who thought it was some crazy publicity stunt thought up to attract them to the circus.

At last, Igon and Valentine threw themselves down on the grass just outside the village, almost completely exhausted. Sweat was running off Valentine's forehead. This was also a new phenomenon to Valentine. Vampires do not perspire or even sweat under any circumstances.

'What does it all mean, Sire?' Igon asked.

'I don't fully understand yet. It started when I bumped my head in my coffin this morning. I somehow knew that I had to get up, no matter what time of day it was. I knew something was that little bit different. I've really felt it since it was thought I had the dreaded Vampire vapours and yet, you see, I knew I didn't have the vapours. I knew I wouldn't, under any circumstances, catch the vapours. I couldn't catch the vapours for one very good reason.'

'What was that, Master?'

'Because, my faithful little friend, I'm not a Vampire. I can't be. Have you ever seen a Vampire's reflection?'

Igon shook his head.

'Have you ever seen a Vampire perspire the way I am right now?'

Igon shook his head again.

'And last, but by no means least, have you ever seen a Vampire walking about in the daylight as I am now? Have you? In all your years of living in the castle, have you ever seen a walking-about-in-the-daytime, perspiring and looking-at-himself-in-the-mirror-type Vampire?'

'Never,' said Igon, a glimmer of understanding coming through. 'Never, never, never.' He was shouting now.

They both stood up and looked at each other with love and understanding.

Igon asked, 'Does this really mean then that you're not a Vampire?'

'I'm sure it does,' Valentine said with a smile a mile wide.

'Then, could the same thing happen to me?' Igon asked, slowly and seriously.

'How could it? You're not a Vampire.'

'Forget about the Vampire bit. I mean, like you, could I ... me ... wake up one morning and find out that I'm not ugly any more. Could that happen to me? Like waking up and finding you're not a Vampire. Could that happen?'

Not for the first time Valentine saw the sadness in Igon's squat, dirty face.

'Well ... er ... I don't see why not,' Valentine answered a little too glibly for the truth.

'I'd like that,' Igon said with a sigh. 'So. What next? What are we going to do now. Go back to the castle and tell the King and Queen that you're not a Vampire?'

'I think not, Igon. I think not. You see, I have a feeling and I don't know why, but I have this feeling that that would not overplease them.'

Igon looked at Valentine and although not really understanding, nodded wisely. It was all too much for him but as he looked into the distance he saw a figure walking along the footpath about a half a mile away, towards the forest.

'That's Wilf. Wilf the Werewolf,' Igon said. 'Should we tell him? Should we shout and tell him you're not a Vampire?'

Valentine put his hand over Igon's mouth. 'No. If that's Wilf, then it's best to let sleeping dogs lie.'

They both laughed out loud, almost loud enough for Wilf to hear.

That night they stayed out of the village and went deep into the forest to sleep and work things out. Valentine had the sneaking feeling that King Victor would soon find out about their disappearance from the castle and would not be too happy about it. He would almost certainly send out the Vampire guards to search for them. If the guards found them they would be taken back to the castle and Valentine would be heavily chastised and punished while Igon, in all probability, would be given to Vernon to play with and do as he wished.

As they slowly walked into the forest, keeping an eye out for trouble – well Igon kept an eye out, Valentine kept them both out – our young hero tried to think back to the days of his early childhood but the only thing he could remember was always being at the castle. Victor was his father, Valeeta was his mother and Vernon was his brother. He could not remember any time of his life when he was not at the castle living with them as a Vampire. He had a vague memory of a childhood fight with Vernon and Vernon lost his temper and said something about '... and I wish you hadn't been brought here', but it was such a long time ago that he couldn't really be sure. They sat down to rest for a while.

'Igon.'

'Master.'

'How long have you lived at the castle?'

'All my life. I was born there.'

'You're human aren't you?'

'Oh yes, Sire. You only have to look at me to see that.'

'How come you were born at the castle?'

'Mummy worked there.'

'What did your ... er ... Mummy do and where is she now?'

'Well, she was a nurse to a Doctor Frankenstein's monster. She used to care for him and get him ready

for bed and, of course, when he needed it, she would also change his oil. Then, as far as I know, she ran away with a man from the circus, the tattooed man.'

'What happened to the monster?'

'She took him with her. They all went with the circus and I've never seen her since.' He wiped a tear from his eye as he always did when he talked about his Mummy. 'I never knew my Daddy,' he continued. 'He was killed. He fell in a vat of wine and, instead of trying to swim, he tried to drink his way out.'

'Good Lord.'

'Yes, he hiccupped to death.'

'Do you remember me being born at the castle?'

'You weren't born at the castle.'

'Go on,' Valentine urged.

'Oh no. One night you weren't there and the next night you were. We were all told you were magic and that you were a special baby but I saw you being brought in by King Victor. You were wrapped in a blanket and he carried you in. That was the only time King Victor came in by the front door and not by the window. He always used the window but not that night.'

Valentine remained silent for a while as he thought over what he had just been told.

'Do you think I was kidnapped; stolen from my real mother?'

'I don't understand.'

'Well, if I was kidnapped, that means that the King isn't my father. The Queen isn't my mother and Vernon is not my brother.'

'Am I still your friend?'

'More than ever,' Valentine smiled.

'Well, that's the only thing that's important to me.'

After a pause of a few minutes Valentine spoke again. 'Igon, we must go deeper into the forest. We have got to get away from Katchem.'

Igon rose from the log.

'Don't you see, Igon. I've got to find out the truth. I've got to find out who I really am.'

'But that's easy. You are Prince Valentine, Knight of the Garter, Knight of the Realm. Last night, tonight and tomorrow night.' Igon spoke with solemnity and more than a touch of pride.

CHAPTER 5

'A President!' the people cry aloud.
King Victor quells an angry crowd.

The moon shone directly on to King Victor's coffin through the open window of his room. Inside the open coffin King Victor opened his eyes and lay there thinking about the daymare he had just had.

After a moment he majestically climbed out of the coffin. But as he stood up he knew that something was out of line. He knew that one or two things would go astray this night. He felt that his biorhythms weren't so good.

There was always one thing that Victor liked about being a Vampire and that was, unlike humans, you didn't have to get dressed when you got up. He was already dressed. He stood there and stretched himself. Then he went into a few late-night exercises. First of all he raised his arms level with his shoulders and

practised a few cloak sweeps. He then did a few deep
breathing exercises, one every four minutes, and
finally sat cross-legged and cross-eyed on the window
ledge with the moon full on his face, trying to get a
little moonburn.

He had a slight headache but he knew that it was
his own fault. He had been sleeping with his top hat
on in his coffin all night and the coffin wasn't long
enough for him and his top hat so it had squashed
down on his forehead. His mother had always told
him, 'Victor, never go to bed with your top hat on,
for two reasons. One, it gives you a headache and,
two, it puts a quiff in your widow's peak.' He felt the
front of his widow's peak and sure enough, there was
a quiff there. Mums are always right.

He had one or two things lined up for the night.
He would start off the evening with a few glasses of
the red stuff at the tavern, but not too many as it
affected his flying. Then, maybe, a little picnic in the
graveyard. Yes, that would be nice.

He glided down from the window ledge and went

over to the hat rack where the last Mayor of Katchem was sleeping. He looked at the bat who was hanging upside down from the hat rack. Victor thought he would scare the old bat so he stood on his head and, with a flick of his fingers, awakened the ex-Mayor. The bat opened its eyes and thought he saw King Victor standing the right way up so he turned over and fell to the floor.

King Victor laughed so hard the moon hid behind a cloud for a moment. He soon had the bat on his shoulder and, knowing that this bat didn't like leaving the room by the window, walked towards the door as if they were going to leave that way. Suddenly King Victor turned round and ran as fast as he could for the window. The bat, whose eyes were almost popping out of its head, dug his little claws into the shoulder of Victor's suit and held on for dear life.

But the King of the Vampires stopped as suddenly as he had started and the impetus took the bat forward and Victor watched him leave the room through the window, alone, as he himself remained firmly in the room.

The ex-Mayor, who was not the best of flyers, fluttered around outside rather like a dragonfly doing its first solo flight. The King, who enjoyed a cruel joke, watched as the bat flew out of control towards the ground. He then left the window and followed the ex-Mayor down. When the bat thought its time had come, Victor dived underneath it and took it safely on to his shoulder.

The bat, who was now so nervous that the fear of flying overtook the fear he had for the Vampire, once more dug his claws into Victor's clothes and grabbed the Vampire's ear with its sharp teeth. King Victor, who was no more than three feet from Queen Valeeta's window, veered with the pain to the left of the window and hit the wall very hard. They both slid down the wall to the ground. The bat let go of his master and flapped his wings as hard as he could to keep himself up in the air. King Victor had nothing to hold on to and continued to slide down the wall to land in the slimy moat below.

Victor's frightening scream was heard the other end of Gotcha, and most of the inhabitants thought that the end of the world had come. He slowly climbed up the damp wall of his castle, making his way to the Queen's window. He gingerly climbed into his wife's room, looking like a not-too-jolly green giant. The Queen, who had been awakened by her

husband's first scream and was now peacefully dropping back into sleep, screamed herself when she saw him.

'Shut up, you silly olt fool,' Victor ordered sharply.

'Who are you?' the Queen asked.

'Your husbant,' Victor said curtly.

'Are you going to a fancy dress ball?'

'No, I'm not goink to a fancy tress ball. If you must know, I fell in the moat.'

The Queen settled back in her coffin, saying, 'Well, you drink too much. That's your trouble. You've been at that bottle of twenty-year-old again, haven't you? I've been watching you lately and you have definitely been coming home well and truly drunk. Every evening we watch you leave by the window heading for the tavern.'

King Victor was looking and feeling a little uncomfortable in his wet clothes.

'And when you get there it's straight for the twenty-year-old bottle. It'll rot your socks, believe me. Look what it did to your father and mother. Your father drank so much twenty-year-old he couldn't fly straight any more and the doctor grounded him, and he was only young. What was he, ninety?'

The green algae was now starting to dry on Victor and his suit was also starting to stiffen up. He only had one change of suit and that was at the cleaners. Valeeta droned on.

'I'll tell you this, Victor. If my mother and father were alive tonight they would turn over in their graves.'

'Vife. You talk too much. I'm goink to see mine children. They should be outside on a beautiful night like this.'

'Vernon is up, down in the cellar. I heard him,' the Queen said.

'Vhat's he doink?' asked the King.

'I'm not sure. I think he's making someone. Go and see if Valentine is out and about. As a matter of fact, I'll come with you.'

The Queen, as beautiful and elegant as ever, rested her arm on that of the beginning-to-pong-a-little King, and together they walked along to Valentine's room.

King Victor softly opened Valentine's door. They crept towards the coffin, expecting him to be asleep. When they discovered the coffin was empty they at first didn't know what to think.

They looked at each other over the open, empty coffin. The Queen looked back into the coffin, not really wanting to look at Victor, while Victor stood there in his now almost green suit, a blue vein quickly pumping on the left side of his white face, his black eyes staring almost unseeing into the coffin. He drew his purple lips back to show his pearl white teeth biting into his pink tongue.

'He's gone,' he hissed. 'He's escaped.'

'How can he escape?' the Queen asked. 'And why should he escape? He's been with us all these years. He knows nothing. Only you and I know how he came here.'

'And Igon?'

'Why should Igon know?'

'Because a fool like Igon knows everythink.'

'Then we are safe. If Igon is a fool who will believe him?'

'Don't spout your female logic at me. The only thing I know is that mine son has escaped. I know he has. I haff a feelink.'

The Queen was not to be intimidated.

'Nonsense. You are talking nonsense. He's probably in his playroom listening to his musical boxes. He's got all the latest ones. Only last week he sent away for Mick Jugular and the Rolling Tombstones.'

'Vy do you prattle on so? Valentine has gone. Vy has he gone? I vill tell you. Somevon in the castle has told him he is not a Vampire. He knows he is not a Vampire. So beink a human child he wants to fint out whom his real parents are and you prattle on about ... er ... Tick Tracular ant the Writhing Twobones.'

'Mick Jugular and the Rolling Tombstones, dear,' his Queen corrected.

The King looked at his wife for a long time before he spoke, as if he was trying to recollect the past events. 'You remember the night I brought him to the castle?'

'Of course,' the Queen said.

'I found him, a small, little thing, not much more than a day old. He vas wrapped up in a blanket vit the vords on a piece of parchment sayink "Please somevon vill you take care off mine little boy," ya?'

'Yes. Look dear. I know all this.'

'But dit you know whom his parents vere, eh?'

'No one did.'

'You are wronk. I dit.'

'How?'

'Because I made it mine duty to find out.'

'Who? Tell me who.' The Queen stared at her husband.

'The Mayor. Ya, Mayor Goop. He vas his father. That is vy I turned him into a bat.'

'And his mother?'

66

'Mrs Goop, who else?' The King was pleased that his wife now knew.

'But why did they leave him?'

'Because then, ven little Valentine vas born, they vere poor, very poor. They had no money at all; notink. They didn't haff two grobbles to rub together. They couldn't afford to keep the child ant don't forget, they also had nine other children. Vhen the tenth von came alonk it vas too much so they hoped that somevon vould find him ant maybe take him in ant look after him. Vich I ... vell ve ... did ant now he is like mine own son only nicer ant better except for runnink avay like this.'

Queen Valeeta smiled at her husband and he took her hand in his saying:

'Go and see if he's in his playroom. I'll alert the servants. I'll see you back here in about twenty minutes, ya?' Victor left the room, closely followed by his Queen.

Everyone in the castle was awakened and asked if they had seen Valentine. They all said no. They were then told to find him, immediately, on pain of death. Candles lit every room in the castle but he couldn't be found and the other mystery was, neither could Igon.

'Vat?' the King bellowed. 'Igon's gone too?' He looked at his other son Vernon and said, 'Vernon, mine other boy, ven ve find Igon he's yours. He's yours to do as you vish.'

Vernon smiled his thanks and rubbed his hands together in eager anticipation. Within minutes torches were lit and the whole of the castle staff made their way to the village.

*   *   *

R.V.—4

Deep inside the forest sat two very tired and lonely men. It was almost black, the trees being so close together that no light penetrated them. Valentine was feeling a mite apprehensive. He was afraid, not of the dark, but of what the King of Vampires might, nay would, do when he realised he had gone.

Victor would now know that Valentine would now know that he wasn't a Vampire and he, Victor, would also know that he, Valentine, would also know that he was kidnapped and smuggled into the castle at a very early age. Victor would know that Valentine would know that by now, because he, Victor, would know that Igon would know and that he, Igon, would tell Valentine.

As for Igon, well, at the moment he knew nothing, as he was hard and fast asleep, probably dreaming of his Mummy. Valentine was very tired, and tomorrow would be the hard day to stay awake, but stay awake he must.

Valentine woke Igon and told him to climb a tree to see if he could see anything unusual going on around them. Igon climbed up the tallest tree near them with surprising agility and soon reached the uppermost branches.

'Can you see anything?' questioned Valentine. He looked up and could see nothing as the tall tree climbed into complete darkness. It was now very dark and Igon at the top of the tree was polishing his glass eye and holding it out towards the village.

'I can see lights, Sire.'

'You'll have to speak up, Igon. I can't hear you. You seem a long way away.'

'Pardon?'

'How far are we from the village?' Valentine cupped his hands and shouted.

'Yes.'

'Yes what?'

'Yes, Sire.'

'Come down Igon.'

'Should I come down, Sire?'

'Yes.'

Pardon?'

'Stay where you are. I'll come up.'

'All right. I'll come down.'

They passed each other half way up or down the tree.

'Igon,' Valentine shouted from the top of the tree.

'Yes Master,' answered Igon loudly from the bottom of the same tree.

Valentine, whose temper was very slow to start, was by now getting a tiny bit agitated with Igon so he counted up to twenty, then another twenty. He eventually reached the figure of fifty-eight before he had his temper under control again. He shouted at the top of his voice, not caring whether anyone else heard him or not.

'I'm going to come down the tree, Igon,' and with that proceeded down the tree as fast as was humanly possible. He was about three-quarters of the way down when he thought something was a bit wrong. He was on a part of the tree that was moving.

Igon spoke. 'Hello Master. Why are you on top of me?'

'Stay where you are, for crying out loud.'

'Me too, Sire. I've been crying out loud but you didn't answer me and you're getting quite heavy, Master.'

'Igon,' said a very tired Valentine.

'Yes, Master?'

'I'm going down to the ground. Will you please follow me.'

'Of course, my Lord.'

Valentine slowly and safely reached the ground.

'Tell me what you saw while you were up this tree, Igon.' Valentine patted the tree they had both climbed.

'Lights, Sire. Many lights. I held my eye out, Sire, and saw many lights all moving in the village.'

'Torches,' Valentine said, almost to himself.

'Yes, torches. Hundreds of them.'

'Then they must have found out that we've left and the King has got the whole village out looking for us.'

'Not good, eh Sire?'

'No, Igon. Not good at all and if he finds us I don't know what he'll do.'

'He'll kill me for starters. Or worse, give me to Vernon.' Igon looked very downcast.

'Don't worry, my old friend. I'll see that he doesn't get either of us,' but Igon noticed there was very little hope in Valentine's voice.

*   *   *

There was tremendous activity at the castle. Everyone had been given a torch and ordered to find Prince Valentine and Igon and bring them back to the castle, alive. Well, one of them was to be alive; Valentine. Victor wasn't too bothered about whether Igon was dead or not; he soon would be.

There was a reward for the man or men who found them and brought them back. The reward was to be a whole day off from work at half pay, or a half a day off from work at full pay.

There was lots of noise and movement, but not much enthusiasm. Almost all of the people of the surrounding villages rather liked Valentine as he wasn't cruel like Vernon or his father. As for Igon, well he was just a harmless character and hardly anybody wanted to see him dead. Not for such a small reward anyway.

Vernon hadn't been as happy since the day he dissected a toad and put its legs on back to front so that when it wanted to jump in the pool or the moat it jumped further away from it. The only way it ended up in the water was to turn away from the place it wanted to jump in and jump in backwards.

He was in the cellar, thinking of the terrible things he could do with Igon.

Queen Valeeta was busy combing her hair and humming an old and traditional Vamparian air to herself.

> *It was a humid Saturday night*
> *The air was still and the moon was bright*
> *The vein was blue and looked so good as the*
> *Vampire sucked the neck of blood.*
> *Tral la lalla lala lah.*

King Victor was in his room in his top hat, string vest and black underpants with the bat motif all over them in white, waiting for his suit to dry. He angrily paced about his room waiting for news of the two escapees.

*   *   *

In the village itself, Doctor Plump bumped into Grabbo and Areta.

'Have you heard the news?' he asked.

'Yes,' said Grabbo and his daughter nodded her lovely head.

'Have you any idea where they might be?' the Doctor asked.

'Not really,' Grabbo said. 'One of the villagers thought he saw what could have been them making towards the woods, but nobody's sure.'

'If anybody knows where find them, I would think that Wilf the Werewolf would,' Areta said nervously.

'Well, let's see if we can find Wilf. Maybe he will tell us,' the Doctor said with more than a glint of greed in his eyes.

'At this time of night Wilf will be in the forest,' Grabbo spoke quietly.

'To the forest then,' Plump said, rubbing his hands together.

'What will you do if you find them there?' Areta spoke firmly.

'Er well . . . what would you do?' the Doctor asked, not wanting to commit himself either way.

'The same as you,' Areta said cleverly. She looked at the Doctor.

The Doctor looked shiftily away from her hard gaze, thinking to himself that if he captured Valentine and Igon he would be in the good books of the King for ever.

'What would you do, Doctor?' she asked again.

'I'm afraid I . . . er, I'd . . .'

'Yes, Doctor?'

'Help them,' he lied.

'So would the whole village,' Grabbo said. 'Nobody wants them hurt. Maybe this is the chance we've all been waiting for, to get rid of the Vampires and elect a president.'

'A president?' the Doctor gulped.

'Yes. The whole of our country is fed up with having a Vampire ruling over us and this may be just the right moment to change all that, wouldn't you think, Doctor?'

'Why yes, of course. Oh yes. A president would be a wonderful idea,' the Doctor lied once more. His thoughts were of a different nature. He was thinking only of himself. He thought that if he captured the two villains now, he would be well in with Victor if the Vampires win. If they lose, I'll be in with the president. Either way I'm in.

'Let's find Wilf,' the Doctor smiled. Actually smiled.

The three of them made off in the direction of the forest. They passed many people pretending to look for Valentine and Igon, but using the excuse to have quick meetings with one another and organise themselves to be ready to strike if called.

They lit up three large torches and made their way into the woods. They went the long way round so as to avoid other people and soon found themselves alone and well on their way, the Doctor thinking of maybe a Vampirehood; Grabbo thinking of who could be president, while Areta thought that the weather that night was doing her hair no good.

*   *   *

King Victor put his suit on although it was still damp. It was also full of wrinkles and creases and looked like the bellows of an accordion. He left as soon as he was dressed, by the window. He made his way to the village and the lights, his temper getting more and more the better of him. His flying that night was not up to his usual standard.

He landed on top of the baker's wife and almost frightened her to death. The lights from the many torches cast evil shadows. The people stood back and sullenly gave him room. One or two of the drunken brave ones were openly hostile to him, but always from a safe distance. Others muttered under their breath. King Victor stood defiantly in the middle of the village, flinging his cloak around the air with all the expertise of a brilliant bull fighter. He was not afraid. He knew the strengths and weaknesses of these puny people. He knew he had the power of magic. He was not afraid of a few sticks or stones. They were harmless compared to the things he could do.

'I am Kink Victor, Kink of all the Vampires ant I am your Master. You, all of you, vill do mine bidding. If you do not, I vill see that you vill live in terror.'

The people were quiet.

'I vill take the youngest son in this village and giff him to Vernon. He can do many things. He can turn your sons into frogs, toads; anythink that takes his fancy. I vill take the younkest boy from the village every day until I get obedience. The Queen ant I ...' It was on the word 'I' that the tomato hit King Victor full in the face with a resounding splat.

The large crowd showed its approval with cheers and cries of 'Capture him.' 'Get him.' 'Tie him up.' 'Let's get the others.' 'We want a president.'

Suffice to say, all these sayings came from the back of the crowd and no one moved towards the King who, although his face was covered with an old tomato, still retained a certain majesty about him. It was while a few agitators at the back were ranting, 'We want a president' that the rest of the people joined in.

Hardly anyone shouted 'Let's kill him,' or 'Do him in.' They didn't really want to kill anyone at the moment. No, they just wanted a president to rule them and this was a Heaven-sent opportunity of letting the Vampires know their feelings. The sound swelled and you could hear 'We want a President' a good two miles away.

'We want a president. We want a president.' Some of the crowd became a little braver and stepped forward, while others were pushed forward from the back by a few cowards who were too afraid to show themselves at the front.

King Victor looked at the circle of people around him; old men and women, a couple of kids, one or two young girls and boys. The trouble was in the thickest part of the crowd.

'A young boy of no more than four years of age, ran towards the King with a small stick in his hand. He raised it to hit the King but his young mother ran out of the crowd and quickly dragged him back to the safety of the crowd. Still from the back came the chanting 'We want a president.' 'Vampires must go.' 'The people rule.'

At the far end of the village came three carts drawn

by fast, but tired, horses from other villages around the area. The carts were full of men; young, fit men, carrying sticks and one or two with axes. Who had sent for these people? They were strangers, yet they were here, all shouting 'We want a president.' 'Death to the Vampires.' 'The People rule.'

Some of them were louts, while a lot of them were drunk. A few shadowy men pointed the way to the trouble then disappeared into the ever-increasing crowd. Eventually the noise and the chanting was almost at its peak with the crowd getting bigger. It also got braver and was now almost touching King Victor. A few more tomatoes and rotten eggs had been thrown but not all had reached their mark. One or two had landed on the public themselves.

King Victor stood perfectly still. He hissed like an enormous snake. Those nearest to him, who felt his breath, afterwards said it was like sulphur. He raised his arms into the air – a typical Vampire pose. The crowd stopped pushing for the moment and Victor turned on a show of Vampire magic that stunned the crowd into silent fear. Not one dog barked; not one child cried; not one person spoke.

The King was in command. He pointed at people

who fell down as if in a faint. He raised a child into the air with one hand, then dropped his hand and the child remained in the air. They gasped as they watched the child float away over their heads.

He hissed. He ranted and he raved. The crowd stepped further away from him. They had never seen power like this before. They had forgotten the stories that their parents had told them about the power of Vampires, as surely as their children would forget the stories that they would tell to them.

Women fainted and strong men ran away. Victor's eyes flashed and dogs and cats squealed and howled in terror.

One drunken man, egged on by other drunken men, ran towards Victor with an axe raised and ready to strike. Victor just stood there and let the man hit him on the neck with a powerful blow. It would have taken the head off any other person, but the axe swung and hit Victor, leaving no mark. The actual force of the blow knocked the axe out of the man's strong hands, but King Victor didn't move. He remained perfectly still. A look of fright entered the drunken man's eyes as he turned and tried to run

back into the crowd and disappear. The crowd opened out for him, making a human lane for him to run down.

Victor took one very deep breath and pointed a long finger at the running man who stopped running and stood on his head in the middle of the crowd. He stood there almost as stiff as a poker, unable to move. Tears of laughter ran down the cheeks of the crowd. Tears of shame ran down the forehead of the upside-down man.

Over the years the villagers had heard of the power of the Vampires, but this was the first time they had witnessed it at such close quarters. The people all more or less thought the same thing at the same time.

'If *he* can do this kind of thing, so can the Queen and so can Vernon and Valentine.'

As if on cue, they started to move away from Victor and the centre of the village and within a few minutes the village street was empty and King Victor was left alone.

He slowly rose in the sky and flew over the village at about thirty feet from the ground. When the people looked up and saw his shape, which had become the shape of an enormous bat, he hovered over them until they had completely disappeared.

CHAPTER 6

Wilf drags Victor from slimy water.
Valentine's in love with Grabbo's daughter.

Igon was once again up the tree, looking towards the
village. He came down, only this time Valentine was
on the ground waiting for him.

'Well?' Valentine asked.

'There seem to be less torches than before but I
thought I saw a few making this way.' Igon looked
worried.

Valentine was looking worried too as he said,
'Somehow we've got to get help, but that might be
difficult in the village. If they think I'm a Vampire
they might not want to help me and if we go further
into the forest we could become hopelessly lost and
maybe even die or be killed by wild animals.'

He looked at Igon who blinked his one eye and
wiped his other one on his sleeve.

'What do you think, Sire, if we stayed here until

things have settled down. Maybe, then, I could go into the village and tell them the truth about you and get help.'

'If we stay here that's as bad as going into the forest,' said Valentine. 'The guards or the villagers would capture us for sure. The King is a very powerful Vampire and he knows every trick in the book. Why, within two nights we would be back inside the castle, me locked in my room and you . . .'

'. . . given to Vernon,' Igon finished the sentence. He continued, 'I think the village is the best hope. Someone might take pity on us and help us escape and get out of the country. We could start a new life. Well at least you could. Wouldn't that be good, Sire?'

'We may be caught in a trap or given back to the King. Or, as you say, we may find someone to help us start a new life. I honestly don't know.'

Valentine sat on a log and tried hard to think clearly for a few minutes. Igon sat thinking with him but what he was thinking about nobody knows.

'Right!' Valentine jumped up. 'We'll go back to the village and see if we can find shelter for a while. Then we will leave late one night and get away from here as far as possible. So . . .' he looked at Igon, 'my old chum. Let's go and see what the future holds for us, my little friend, shall we?'

'Yes. Let's do that.' Igon put his hand in that of Valentine's and whispered, 'Friend,' and off they both went to the village.

They hadn't travelled more than a few hundred yards when they met Grabbo, Doctor Plump and Areta, who, to Valentine, was the most beautiful thing he had ever seen in his entire, although admittedly sheltered, life. His eyes lit with pure joy as they looked into hers.

He explained to them what had happened to himself and Igon and looked straight at Areta when he told them that he was not a Vampire. She was so thrilled that Valentine thought he saw tears in her wonderful eyes, but in the light of the torches he couldn't be sure.

Grabbo offered them shelter for a short while. There was a cellar under his tavern that very few people knew about, so they could stay there. It was only left to get them through the village without being seen or captured.

Valentine thanked him, while Doctor Plump tried to smile and say that he was sure everything would turn out fine, but he couldn't look Valentine in the eyes, or anyone else for that matter. He was busy working out how he could get a message to the King that he knew where Valentine and Igon were.

The small group made their way back to the village very carefully, not realising that Wilf the Werewolf was following them a few yards behind, and wondering whether to turn them in or help them. When they had almost reached the village, the Doctor made his excuses and said that he had to get back to his surgery as he had one or two things to attend to.

The group wished him well and watched him make his way back to his surgery, or so they thought as he turned the corner and became lost to their sight.

Dr Plump stopped for a moment, but he didn't see Wilf hiding in a doorway a few yards away. Wilf had decided to follow the Doctor. The Doctor now looked around to make sure he couldn't be seen by his friends and stealthily made his way to the castle.

*   *   *

'Come in,' the Queen said, looking towards the door.

A rather pale, sad and dishevelled Ronnoco entered the Queen's chambers. He had been let out of prison on the promise that he wouldn't be found drunk in the street again. They didn't believe him when he told the police that he had fainted.

'Your Majesty, the Doctor is here to see you.'

'Why? I'm not ill am I? One's never too sure these days.'

'He says he has a message about Prince Valentine.'

'Oh, I see,' she said, greatly relieved that she wasn't ill. 'Well, tell him he must give it to His Majesty the King.' She put the hairbrush down on the dressing table. It was very difficult for Ronnoco to look at her sitting at her dressing table, combing her hair without the aid of a mirror. He also thought it must be very difficult for her too.

'I'm afraid, Your Majesty, that the King isn't in the castle. He's . . . er . . . flying over the village and I won't be able to tell him,' Ronnoco said, looking and feeling rather confused.

'What's he flying as?' the Queen snapped.

'A bat, Marm.'

'A small one or a big one?'

'A very big one.'

'Oh dear, if he's a very big one, he's really lost his temper. That means "look out".' She turned her back on Ronnoco, dismissing him with a wave of her hair brush. She started to comb her hair once more, looking very intently into the mirror that wasn't there.

Ronnoco stood where he was for a few seconds, not really knowing what to do. No more conversation came his way so he quietly left the room.

83

The Queen stopped combing her hair and looked at where the mirror should have been and gave a satisfied smile that seemed to say she liked what she couldn't see. She patted her hair and gently shook her head, letting her hair fall into its natural style.

She rose from her dressing table and walked sedately over to the window and looked out. In the distance she saw a large, very large, bat flying over the village. She cupped her hands together, took an enormous breath and with a tremendous effort that almost made her dizzy, shouted:

'Victorrrrr!'

She watched the shadow stop in mid-flight and she knew then that he had heard. She continued her shouting.

'Coome innn attt onceee, there'sss someeeonee heree toooo seee youuuu,' and with that she shut the window and watched the shadow make its way back from the village.

'Good Dracula, he's overdoing the bat tonight,' she thought. Once more she sat at her dressing table and with great difficulty put on a fresh lipstick.

A tremendous fluttering broke her concentration. She looked towards the window, her lips still puckered from putting on the lipstick, and saw Victor trying to get in. Unfortunately, he was too large to get in through the window. She ran to the window and opened it as wide as she could.

'Oh, dear,' she said with more than a touch of annoyance in her voice. 'What *are* you doing? Why aren't you here when you're wanted, and what are you doing scaring the whole village to death? Why have you made yourself into such a big bat? You look quite ridiculous. Really Victor, it's too much. People

84

will think you're quite mad. You know that, don't you? They'll think you're quite mad. It will take hours to get down to a reasonable size. Anyway, the Doctor ... Victor! Are you listening?'

Victor was trying his best to listen and his hardest to keep in the air.

'The Doctor wants to see you. He has a message for you about Valentine.' She went back into her room.

Victor was losing his strength, trying to keep his enormous wings going. He was fighting a losing battle. Slowly but surely he was sinking to the ground with his wings flapping hard enough to cause a small gale. Eventually he had to give in and he fell the last twenty feet with a splash into the moat below.

He floated on top of the green, slimy water looking like a large broken kite. His small, weak cries for help were heard by Queen Valeeta who looked out of the window down to the moat and in a loud and unladylike voice shouted down to her unfortunate husband:

'It serves you right, you silly old fool!' She then closed the window and bolted it.

Wilf, who was standing behind a tree, watched Victor and heard Valeeta. He shouted across the water, 'Victor ... Hey, Victor. Come on old lad; come on over to this side of the moat. I'll get you out.'

Victor did his best. His little bat legs were doing the bat crawl for all they were worth.

'That's it, Vic old pal. Keep going. You'll make it.'

Victor got to about three feet from the bank where Wilf was now standing, but the poor Vampire was almost exhausted.

'Come on, son. Just a bit more,' Wilf shouted and jumped up and down.

Victor gave one final effort to reach the bank for the last time.

'Come on, Vicky boy. Let's be having you,' Wilf encouraged, and then quickly grabbed the tip of Victor's wing before he went down for the third time, and slowly dragged him to the safety of the bank. As Victor lay there, doing his utmost to breathe, Wilf tried to clean off the slime that was covering poor King Victor.

'By golly, Vic, you're big. I've never seen a bat as big as you before. Come to think of it, I've never seen anything as big as you before. How come you're so big?'

Wilf realised that Victor, being a bat and a very tired one at that, couldn't speak, so he patted him on his head saying, 'I'll stay with you till you get back to normal.'

Victor belched as a two pound carp looked out of his mouth. Wilf, being a kindly werewolf, gently took it out of the bat's mouth and put it back into the moat and watched it dive in the slimy, but safe, water.

*　　*　　*

Valentine and Igon were now ensconced in the safety of Grabbo's cellar below the tavern, eating food provided by Grabbo and served by Areta, with whom Valentine had fallen madly, head-over-heels in love.

Igon was eating the food as if tomorrow was going to be a fast. Grabbo stood alone in a corner of the cellar and watched both Valentine and Igon until they had finished eating. A bottle of wine had been produced and as the two men drank, Grabbo spoke.

'Well, Sir,' he addressed Valentine. 'What do you have in mind?'

'In mind, Sir?' asked Valentine. 'How do you mean?'

'Well, what I mean is, what are you going to do? Are you really going to leave the country, providing you can get help, or are you going to stay and help us?'

'Help who?' Valentine finished his drink.

'Us. The people of the village; the country as a whole.' Grabbo moved towards him.

'I'm sorry, I don't quite understand.' Valentine looked at Grabbo.

'We need someone like you. Someone who understands. Someone who has had an education; had an upbringing. Someone who can deal with people and problems, and, most of all, someone who is young and eager.' Grabbo put another box next to Valentine and sat down.

He carried on. 'You see, Sir. If I can be honest with you ...' Valentine nodded. 'We, that is the village, even the country as a whole, is how can I say fed up? Being ruled by Vampires.' Grabbo's face was pale and nervous, his eyes darting around the room but always coming back to Valentine. 'We want someone to be our first ... our first ... er ... president.' He rose quickly and walked away from Valentine and carried on speaking.

'What we want we being the people is someone to lead us forward into the future. Someone clever enough to get the best out of the people and help them. Someone we can trust but who can also be firm if needs be, and will treat us kindly too.' Grabbo came back and sat on the box next to Valentine again as Igon hiccupped.

'You see, Sir. What I'm trying to say is that if you

88

were to be our president, I know the rest of the people would follow you. I'm sorry if I'm not putting the proper words together but could you think about it?' Here he trailed off and looked at Valentine.

There was a silence, broken only by the sound of Igon scratching his head.

'Do you understand what I'm asking, Sir?'

Valentine gently put the wine glass down, wiped his mouth on a handkerchief and said, 'Yes, I think I do, Grabbo. What you're saying is that you – not necessarily the people, but at the moment *you* – want me to lead you forward into the future, while at the same time getting the best out of the people. Also, I should imagine, that you will want me to get rid of the Vampires, who educated me, brought me up, looked after, and in their way loved me. Am I right, Grabbo?' Valentine smiled at him, then quickly looked at Areta and smiled at her too.

Igon belched as Grabbo said, 'I think so, Sir. I'm not too sure, but I think so, Sir. But you know what will happen to you if you are caught by King Victor, don't you? You will be killed. I will be killed. Areta will be killed . . .'

'I will be, I know that,' Igon sighed, 'or given to Vernon.'

'I don't think King Victor would kill me but maybe you are right about yourself and Igon, although I will say this – that in no way would I let them harm one hair of Areta's head.' Valentine stood up and held Areta's hand in his.

Grabbo looked pleased. Almost as pleased as Areta herself.

'Let me think about it, Grabbo. Give me a few days to think it over.'

89

'A few ... Sir, there isn't a few days left. You must make your decision now. I could get a message to the people very quickly. They are not happy at the moment and they are going to turn ugly.'

'I always have been,' Igon said quietly. Areta patted Igon on the cheek.

Valentine quickly finished his glass of wine and walked around the room. By the expression on his face you could see he was thinking very deeply but his biggest worry was how to get Victor and his family out of the castle without hurting them. After all, they were the only parents he had known and they had really been very kind to him, especially the Queen who, up till twenty-four hours ago, as far as he was concerned was his Mother.

'Grabbo?'

'Sir?'

'If, and I repeat, if, I decided to become president and the people accept me, of course, I must make one condition. No harm must come to the Vampires – not even Vernon.'

'Pity,' Igon mumbled.

'The people won't like that, Sir. They will want to kill the Vampires.'

'You can't kill a Vampire, you know that.'

'You can with a stake.'

'Oh yes,' Igon interjected. 'You can kill a Vampire with a stake, or a lamb chop if you put enough poison on it.' He laughed.

'You can't kill a Vampire with poison, Igon. You, of all people, should know that. Within a few years he will come back to life again. Time means nothing to a Vampire.' Valentine spoke firmly to Igon who looked a little ashamed.

Valentine went on. 'I will not allow any harm to come to them.'

Grabbo thought for a moment. 'I shall have to put it to the people and see what they say. I shall do my best but I don't think they will be very happy. Already they are shouting for blood. I know what they are thinking. Tomorrow when it's light they will go to the castle and while the Vampires are asleep in their beds . . .'

'Coffins,' Igon corrected.

'Pardon?'

'Coffins. Vampires sleep in coffins,' Igon said with authority.

'Oh. In their coffins. They will put stakes in their hearts and kill them. Of that there is no argument.'

Grabbo looked nervous. Valentine looked perturbed. Igon looked silly. Areta looked beautiful.

'As I have already said, Grabbo, if I become this country's first president I will insist that no harm comes to them. I only ask that I be allowed to talk to them. If anybody can, I must be able to talk to them and maybe show them the errors of their ways.'

Grabbo slowly nodded and put his strong arm around his daughter Areta who lifted her face towards her father and smiled.

'You must try to explain to the people, Father,' she said.

'Very well. I will talk to a few of the elders and see if I can make them understand your arguments and your beliefs. I can't promise, but the least we can do is try. So, come, my friends, let's go and meet the people.'

They left the cellar and carefully made their way to the street above, which, now that King Victor had left, was beginning to show signs of life again. People were coming back into the streets, some of whom were carrying sticks that had been shaped into stakes. Grabbo gathered a few people around him and began to speak.

* * *

Wilf had helped Victor back into the castle through the front door. Vernon was in his lab, madly mixing steaming, bubbling vials of different colours and chuckling insanely, his eyes alight with the hope of using them on Igon, or anyone else for that matter, but on Igon first.

The Queen was trying to get Victor into his coffin. He had almost returned to normal. By that, you could see that he wasn't a bat any more. He was back to his immaculate self, except for his legs which were still the legs of a bat. At the moment he was hanging upside down underneath the table on which his coffin rested. The Queen knelt down and talked to him.

'Victor, you must try and get your legs back. You look positively foolish with your bat legs. If anyone came in now and saw you, I wouldn't know where to put myself, I honestly wouldn't.'

'I'm concentratink as hard as I can, mine dear, but it vas a bik strain turnink into such a huge bat.'

'Excuse me,' Wilf said from the window, 'Er ... I don't want to cause you any anxiety, but there's a lot of people milling about in the village.'

The Queen walked over to the window and looked out. She arched her eyebrows, flared her nostrils, looked at Wilf and asked, 'Have you got mange?'

'No, I don't think so. Why?'

'Because you are dropping fur all over my carpet.'

'Ah yes. Well, I'm very sorry, but, you see, what's happening is I'm slowly turning back to normal.'

'Wilf,' Her Majesty said, 'I don't think you have ever been normal. No one in this village, or even in this country, is normal. If it wasn't for Victor, Valentine, Vernon and myself, this whole country would be inhabited by mad people.'

Wilf didn't really listen to the Queen's speech as he was too busy picking up bits of fur that were falling off him at an alarming rate.

'I think I ought to be leaving now,' he said, clutching an armful of fur. 'You see, I promised Mum a fresh loaf.'

There was a sudden scream from under the coffin table. As they looked at where Victor was hanging

upside down they noticed that his left leg was back to normal but his right leg was still that of a bat.

'Keep concentrating dear,' the Queen encouraged.

Wilf left the room, picking up his fur, but it was a difficult task. As fast as he picked one patch up, another patch fell off him.

The Queen watched Wilf leave the room. As the door shut she turned to her growing husband and in an acid voice she asked:

'Why is that Wilf person so familar? Why does he talk to you that way?' She looked under the coffin table to make sure she had been heard, and continued. 'Big buckets of blood. He calls you by your first name. He actually calls you Victor or Vicky and I've even heard him call you Vic. Why do you allow this?'

King Victor, although in a certain amount of growing pain and extremely tired, said with a long sigh, 'Mine dear, I vill tell you. The reason I allow him, ant only him, to call me Victor or Vicky, or even Vic, is because in a vay he is von off us. Although he is not a Vampire, like you ant I, every now and again he turns into a Verevolf.

The holidaymakers come here in their thousands ant spend lots of money of vich ve get our share, but the person they come to see is Vilf. Ya, Vilf the Verevolf. They talk to each other: "Haff you seen Vilf the Verevolf?" they say. "No, vot is he like?" they ask. "Oh, he is vonderful ant he doesn't mind if you stroke him." So, mine dear, he brings in a tremendous amount of money.

The other reason I allow him this privilege is because tonight vas the second time he has saved mine life. Vile I vas drownink in the vater of the moat, who vas it that came to mine rescue, eh? Whom vas

94

it? Vernon maybe? No. Mine vife maybe? No. Mine servants maybe? No.

Vilf. Ya, that's right, Vilf the Verevolf. He came to save me. So, mine little von, instead of givink him a medal for all the money he brinks here and for two times saving mine life, I allow him to call me Victor, or Vicky, or even Vic. That is not a bad price to pay, is it mine precious?'

The Queen walked out of the room without answering. As far as she was concerned, he was a King and should, by all accounts, be treated as one by all his subjects, whether they save lives or make money. 'That was the way I was brought up. Always to respect your King.'

CHAPTER 7

Victor and Vernon in a contest of magic;
if Victor loses, for Igon it's tragic.

When Grabbo told the crowd in the square about
Valentine saying yes, he would become their first
president, there was a tremendous cheer. Grabbo
then asked Valentine to talk to them. He was lifted
on to a cart so that he could be seen above the crowd
as well as being heard.

'My friends,' he started. 'First of all, may I say how
proud I am to be asked to be your first president.'

Loud cheers.

'Until recently I believed I was a Vampire ...'

A hush.

'... but you can imagine what a great thrill it was
for me when I found out I'm not a Vampire.'

Louder cheers than before.

'It will not be easy.'

Lots of heads shaking.

'I want you to be happy.'

Louder cheers than the second loud cheers.

'I cannot do this alone. I will need someone by my side. Someone to share the worries and the burden of office.'

Lots of surprised faces looked at each other.

'I think I have found that person who will be my help.'

'The person I am talking about is a woman.'

All the males looked at all the females.

'And she is here tonight.'

Lots of necks stretched and strained, and all eyes widened.

'I am asking Areta to be my wife.'

There were even louder cheers than the third lot of loud cheers.

Areta was almost thrown on to the cart next to Valentine. He held her hand. She was smiling yet shaking with excitement.

'Yes, yes, yes,' the crowd shouted.

She looked softly at Valentine and demurely nodded her head. He kissed her gently. The cheering was now louder than all the other cheering put together. The crowd started chanting.

'Long live the President Valentine and Areta!'

Valentine held his hand up for a moment's silence, but the crowd were ecstatic and would not be made quiet.

'God bless you, Valentine,' they all shouted.

'Free at last!'

'No more Vampires!'

'Death to the Vampires!'

'To the castle and kill the lot of them!'

The crowd started to move. They picked up hammers and stones; knives were sharpened; stakes - even scythes - were seen.

'Wait! Please wait!' shouted Valentine but his voice went unheard. Within a few hectic seconds there was only Valentine, Areta, Grabbo and Igon left in the village square. The uncontrollable mob were on their way to the castle.

'Please stop,' Valentine shouted after the last few running towards the main body of the crowd. 'Don't harm them. Let me talk to them ...' But he soon realised he was shouting in vain.

Wilf, now almost normal except for a few patches here and there, and wearing a sheet from the castle, was on his way back to the village when he saw the great crowd coming up the hill, still chanting 'Death to the Vampires'. He hid behind a tree and watched as they marched past. Then he saw the baker, Ari Hovis, in the crowd and sprang out to grab him.

'What's going on?' he asked.

'We're going to kill the Vampires,' Ari shouted excitedly.

'I hope you know what you're doing. Anyway, is your shop open? I promised Mum I'd take her home a fresh loaf.'

The crowd swept on as the baker shouted back, 'Help yourself, Wilf. The brown ones are the freshest. Pay me the next time you see me.'

Wilf stood alone in the middle of the path and watched the crowd snake up the hill to the castle. He thought to himself, 'I hope Mum's not in that lot.'

*　　*　　*

The Doctor was hurried into the King of the Vampire's chamber.

'Vell, Doctor. Vot is it? I'm a very busy man.'

The Doctor looked at Victor whose right leg was six inches shorter than his left one. Or, thought the Doctor, maybe his left leg is six inches longer than his right one.

'Hurry, man. Vot is it?'

'I know where Prince Valentine is,' he blurted out.

'Vere?' the King shouted as he jumped up and overbalanced.

'He's with Grabbo in a secret cellar,' the Doctor said. The King, for safety's sake, was now sitting on the floor. 'They are plotting against you.' The Doctor allowed himself a small smirk.

'Vere is this secret cellar, you oaf?' Victor shouted, as he rose up on one leg. The Doctor looked a trifle hurt at being called an oaf.

'Under the tavern.'

King Victor turned his back on Doctor Plump and put his hand over his mouth to muffle a short scream as the amazed Doctor watched Victor's right leg grow very quickly to its full size. The King turned round and gave the mystified Doctor a sickly grin.

'Come,' the King said, 've must go to the tavern ant if ve capture mine son, Valentine, I vill never forget you, ya?' He patted the Doctor on the throat. Doctor Plump nervously gulped air as he wondered what the King of the Vampires meant by that last remark.

*   *   *

Vernon, who was as mad as the proverbial January, February and March Hare, was in his cellar looking

100

at a very old and dusty book on Black Magic. The cellar was thick with green steam, black smoke, pink bubbles and a bright blue, rather pretty, froth that was slowly but surely making its way across the ceiling. From the book he read aloud:

'Four hairs from a Chinaman's pigtail,
The eye of a completely dead fish.
You must boil them in oil for an hour,
Drink it and then make a wish.
Your wish will come true if you do this,
If the Chinaman comes from Hong Kong.
If he doesn't, it's not worth trying;
I'm afraid that your wish will go wrong.
Chorus
Oh, I'm from Gotcha
Yes, I'm from Gotcha
Where the Vampires rule
And bite your lily white neck."

Anonymous. 9th century.

He flicked the pages quickly as if he knew on which page to find the magic potion he was looking for. Suddenly his eyes lit up. 'Ah,' he exclaimed. A sound came from his throat that was the nearest he could make to laughter. 'Yes.' He started to laugh again. 'This is the one. I knew it was in this special book of magic. Wonderful. Wonderful!' Tears of joy and anticipation escaped from his small, pig-like, black eyes. He read aloud again:

How to turn the ugliest of things (including people) into stone.
They will not be able to move, but they will not be dead.
You will need the skin of a yellow chameleon.
The sting of a two-week-old bumble bee.

101

2 oz yeast.

Sixty-one hairs from an antelope's tail (please note - only sixty-one. This is important. You are recommended *not* to count the hairs near a window or draught).

A crushed ruby (large) from a prince's crown

1 oz of warts

He read on and on, knowing that he had everything that the book asked for; even more in case of spillage. He finished reading, took a deep breath, sat down and relaxed for a few moments, stroking his two-headed dog on its left head while watching the right head look on with envy. As he sat there, meditating on what he would do with Igon, the Queen strode majestically into the cellar. She found her son still stroking the two-headed dog.

She thought, 'How cruel of Vernon to call one head Fang and the other head Bruce.' That meant when he called Fang, Bruce had to come too.

Vernon saw his mother looking at a placard leaning against the wall with the words 'Vernon bites yer throat'.

'Yes, Mother?' he said, hating to be disturbed in what he thought was really his domain.

'Ah, Vernon. Have you seen your father?'

'Many times, I'm afraid,' he quipped.

'Do not make jokes about your father, Vernon. You know he loves you.'

'I know nothing of the kind. Anyway, that's beside the point. There's very little difference between love and hate.'

The Queen nervously removed some non-existent dust off her sleeve.

'What does Daddy want?' Vernon asked with a smirk.

'Help,' she answered. 'He needs all the help he can get. Yours too, Vernon. I presume you know what's going on out there, don't you dear?' she pointed first to the wall and then to the ceiling, suddenly realising there were no windows.

'Of course I do,' said Vernon. 'I tried to tell him this would happen but did he believe me? He did not. He didn't even listen, he laughed. So now there's trouble and who's the first person he turns to for help? Me. Little old Vernon, his beloved son.' He stroked Fang's head so hard with temper that even Bruce's eyes watered.

'Your father knows nothing about this,' insisted his mother. 'If he thought I was here, asking for your help, he would be most upset.'

'Good. And I'll tell you something else, Mother dear. He can't have my help. I wouldn't help him if he was the last Vampire on earth.' Vernon was getting very worked up. He picked up a rubber ball from the floor and threw it across the room. He shouted, 'Fang, fetch! Bruce, stay!'

The two-headed dog fell to the ground, each trying to obey its master's command.

'Vernon, you worry me. You really do. Your Daddy and I have tried to bring you up as a perfect Vampire. We want you to be happy and, as you know, one day you will rule this land. Your dear Daddy has tried so hard and he wants you to follow in his heart beats.' A small tear ran down the Queen's cheek but it made no impression on Vernon.

'Close the door when you leave, please. I'm working on a plan for Igon. One slight mistake and it will go wrong.' He kicked the two-headed dog who was now trying to fight itself on the floor.

'Well!' said the Queen, quite hurt by his tone. She left the cellar, closing the door.

*   *   *

Valentine was saddened by what he had seen of the villagers. It hurt him to think that they were making their way to the castle to try and kill the only family he had known. But there seemed to be so little he could do. He could warn them, of course.

He was also worried about the villagers themselves. He knew the power of the Vampire and the range of their magic. Many people would get hurt, even killed. He turned to Areta.

'I think I should try and stop the villagers and if not, at least warn the King and Queen and ask them

104

not to harm the villagers too much. I'm sure they will listen to me, which is more than the people here did.'

'I'll come with you.'

'No, dearest. I don't think you should. Stay here with your father. Igon and I will give ourselves up to the Vampires and that way maybe we will be able to get together and talk to each other. That must help all of us.' He squeezed her hand.

'You are very brave. Please be careful, my love.' She walked over and stood by her father. Grabbo held his hand out towards Valentine and they shook hands.

'Be careful, my boy.'

'I will, I promise.' With a nod to Grabbo, he looked once more at Areta and then made his way with Igon towards the retreating villagers.

The first person they met was Wilf.

'Hello,' he said. 'Have you heard that they are all going up to the castle to try and kill the Vampires? What for, I say? Well, I mean, if they do that they might think about doing me in the next time I change into a werewolf.' Wilf looked downcast.

'We're going to try and stop them. Come and join us, Wilf, will you?'

'Ah. I can't at the moment. You see, I promised Mum a fresh loaf and I've had a word with Ari and he said his shop is open and to help myself.'

'Well, Wilf. If they do you in, that loaf of bread isn't going to be much good, is it?' Igon spoke for the first time in a long time. He had been trying very hard to think, but it was a slow, hard process for him.

'Look. I tell you what. I'll go home and change, pick up a loaf, then I'll come along up to the castle. How do you feel about that?'

'That's fine, Wilf.' Valentine smiled. 'We'll see you there.'

'Right,' said Wilf and made his way to the village as Valentine and Igon trudged on to the castle.

The crowd was now outside the castle gates, facing the big doors. They were chanting and telling all the people in the castle why they were there.

*   *   *

'Dearest,' the Queen spoke softly. 'What are you going to do about those people down there? The ones who are shouting for your blood.'

'Fetch Vernon,' the King answered.

'He won't come.'

'I command him to come.'

'He's sulking.'

'Oh,' said the King, nonplussed. He had never been refused a command before and now that he had for the first time in his life, he didn't know what to do.

'Vot should I do then, Doctor, eh?' the King asked.

The Doctor looked at everyone in a highly nervous state. 'Er ... I ... er ... yes. Er ... I ... well, er ... maybe ...' The Doctor's voice petered out to an inaudible whisper.

'How about you?' The King pointed to Ronnoco. 'Vat do you think I should do, ya?'

Ronnoco gave a frightened grin. The King looked gently at his beautiful Queen and, with a catch in his seemingly distant voice, said, 'Is this the end off little Victor?'

'No dear. Not if you do as I tell you.'

'I'm listenink,' he said in a very tired voice.

'Well, first of all, you have to make your mind up that you're not going to be King any more.'

106

'But ... I ...' The King started to interrupt.

'Let me finish,' the Queen went on. 'I think you've been King long enough. How long? The last hundred and five years?'

He nodded.

'Now, why don't you let Vernon, or even Valentine, be King. Then you and I can get away from this terrible castle and buy a nice little cottage in the country and if you like, we could have a small flat.'

'A small, flat vat?' the King asked.

'A small flat. An apartment. Here in Katchem. You'd like that. No more worries. No affairs of State. Think of it, dear. Why, you'd be able to write that book you're always on about. What were you going to call it?' she asked proudly.

'*Gone vith the Bat*' he answered sheepishly.

The Queen stopped speaking and watched her very tired husband think. He took his top hat off and polished it with his beautifully manicured hands. He put it back on his head at a rather jaunty angle.

'Well?' Valeeta asked.

'Vot do you think, Doctor?'

'Er well. I ... er. If ... er ... Maybe ...'

'I'm very tired, I must say. Ant the idea off retirink is lookink pleasant.' He climbed out of his coffin.

The Queen, who knew she was getting to her husband, put out more feelers for him to latch on to.

'Don't forget,' she said, 'You'll be able to go to the pub with your cronies. People like Wilf the Werewolf and Dick the Big Daft Dwarf. You like them, don't you? And you could drink your twenty-year-old to your heart's content as you wouldn't have the worries of State weighing heavily on your shoulders. And

107

you'll be able to do the garden. I can see you now, planting some flowers in the moonlight. And, maybe, in a few years' time, we will have grandchildren running around the house all night.'

She waited to see if her little plan had worked. In the background they could hear the villagers' voices getting louder as they came closer.

'Get Vernon,' the King ordered, 'and get him now. Tell him if he isn't here in the next few minutes he vill never be Kink.'

The Queen gave a small sigh of relief. 'Yes dear. I'll go and get him now.'

As she left the room Ronnoco heard the crowds chanting for the blood of the Vampires and, he thought, anyone who worked for them, so he did the only thing he was very good at. He fainted.

'Doctor,' the King said. 'Just look at that fool. He's fainted again.' He kicked Ronnoco with the point of his shoe. 'Can't you help him, Doctor?'

'Er . . . well . . . er. I . . . er . . . maybe.' The Doctor burst into tears. Victor looked at them both with disdain and walked over to the window.

He looked down on the moving torches and the chanting crowd. He smiled to himself, knowing that with one flick of his fingers he could have them all running back to their homes with panic on their ugly faces. He thought hard about doing it, then thought better of it. 'Maybe Valeeta's right' he thought. 'Maybe I should retire ant get away from trouble like this. Who vants these problems?' His eyes softened as his thoughts wandered

'The pub with the lads every Saturday night. Moonlit football. Gettink to bed early, maybe four or five in the morning. Sounds vonderful.' These thoughts were broken as the door burst open and his Queen dragged Vernon in by his ear.

'Vernon, mine son. So glat you could come, ya?'

'What is it you want, Father? Mother has been mumbling something about you abdicating and me being King. Good. Because I would make a better King than you. Igon would make a better King than you.

First of all, I would kill everyone who had anything to do with this rebellion, but I would torture them first. Igon – he's the one I want. Every day I would change him into something different. A frog. A three-legged dog. A stone gnome. A crow with a broken wing. No, two broken wings. Ha ... ha ... ha ...'

He laughed like a man possessed of the Devil, which, of course, he was. The King looked at his wife as if to say 'Vhere did ve go vrong?' His wife clipped Vernon around the ears with a resounding slap. Vernon screamed. The Doctor, whose eyes were still streaming with tears, also let out a scream. A very loud and a very high one. The chanting was getting louder and louder and closer and closer.

'Vernon. Listen to me ant listen gut because I'm only goink to say this vonce. I vos goink to abdicate the throne ant let you become Kink but I'm afraid you are not vise enough or clever enough or votever else enough. You are a cruel boy ant I'm goink to teach you a lesson. I challenge you now to kill me vith any off your magic. If you do, then in front off these vitnesses I vill say you must be Kink. But, if you fail ant I am not kilt, you must leave the country ant go abroad ant never set feet int this country again. Do you understant?'

109

Vernon's cruel twisted mouth curled into a sinister grin. He quickly and gladly nodded his head, bowed to his mother and father, clicked his heels and asked for permission to leave the room to get his magic set. It was given. He ran to his cellar with the speed of a bullet.

*   *   *

Valentine and Igon had caught up with the crowd and were now leading them. Every few steps they tried to stop the people and talk some sense into them but the crowd would have none of it. Forward, ever forward, seemed to be their motto.

'Please let me talk to the Vampires. Let me speak to them. They know me. They will listen to me. I was their son. I'm sure they will listen to me.'

But the crowds wouldn't listen to him. Valentine was almost carrying Igon in their efforts to keep up with them.

*   *   *

Back in the King's chamber came Vernon, carrying a phial of foaming liquid: 'Are you ready?' he asked his father.

'I am,' said Victor proudly.

'Victor, please . . .' pleaded the Queen.

'Do not vorry, mine sveetness.' He smiled at his wife.

Vernon once more clicked his heels and drank a little of the potion. He immediately blew a long flame of fire from his mouth, directly towards his father's face. His father had seen this trick many years before. Half a second was all that Victor needed. He took a breath so powerful and so deep, and then blew at the

110

approaching flame with such ferocity that the flame was actually turned round in its path and flew across the room in an entirely different direction.

It flew over an awakening Ronnoco who, as he tried to stand up, felt the top of his head being well and truly singed so he fainted again. The Doctor almost joined him as he saw the flame shoot across the room. The King smiled at his son.

Vernon looked at his father with hate and once more ran downstairs, this time without asking for permission to leave and with no click of the heels.

The village people were now in the castle itself, but no one knew the way to the Vampires' rooms.

Victor was holding his wife firmly by the throat when Vernon came back into the room. As Vernon knew, for a Vampire to hold someone's throat as Victor was doing, was a sign of tremendous love and affection. After all, they had been married for over ninety-nine years.

Vernon half clicked his heels and drank from the new phial. Victor looked at the colour of the liquid. That told him something. He then looked at the eyes of his son as he drank, to see whether or not the liquid affected his pupils. He looked also at the colour of his skin to see if it changed even minutely. Putting all these things together in his mind, like a flash of lightning, he worked out the physical antidote, and how to use it to see that as little harm as possible came to himself.

Vernon drank the fluid and before you could say 'Katchem for the Cup' he had grown to the size of a giant. He was at least eleven feet tall. The most fascinating thing was that his clothes also grew in a corresponding size. The Queen looked at her

enormous son and thought how wonderful he looked, being so tall and quite handsome.

Victor braced himself for what he knew was about to happen to him. Vernon walked over to his father with the cocksure intention of just picking him up and throwing him to the ground, breaking every bone in his body.

Vernon gripped his father round the waist but, to his surprise, he found that he couldn't even lift him off the ground, let alone throw him on to it. So he decided upon a different ploy and tried to squeeze the breath out of his father. But the King was a shrewd opponent and had seen a lot in his long life. In no way was he going to be fooled.

Vernon strained and moaned and grunted but eventually had to give up. He once again ran out of the room to his cellar.

The Queen looked at her husband and said, 'Didn't you think he looked handsome when he was tall? I thought he was really very good looking, didn't you, dear?'

'Yes. I must be honest. I thought beink tall suited him better than not beink it.'

CHAPTER 8

A two-headed dog; a beetle of stone.
Igon stretched out, all alone

A large crowd had gathered in the hall of the castle, after forcing their way in. In the front of the crowd stood Valentine and Igon. The few guards present there were at a loss. They didn't know what to do. They didn't want to harm the villagers because they were villagers themselves. Why, some of them even had relations standing in front of them.

Valentine tried to quieten the mob that, unfortunately, was being led and urged on by a few people whose only thought was to cause trouble, not to try and find a solution. There were shouts of 'This way!' and 'That way!' or 'Where are they?' and 'Let's kill them'. But no one was taking a positive lead. No one was actually saying 'This way, men'.

So they milled around the castle hall, talking and shouting, but mainly arguing with each other. Already a couple of fights had broken out.

Valentine stood on the only table, shouting at the top of his voice, 'Listen to me, please.'

One man shouted, 'Speak up.'

Another said, 'Keep quiet.'

A couple of older people at the back shouted out to let the new President elect speak. Gradually a certain amount of order was restored. Valentine spoke.

'Friends, you are in my home. Yes, my home. The only place I've ever known. The place I love. The place I was brought up in. Yes, friends, this is my home and you are now in it. You are uninvited but you are here. You ...' and he pointed at certain people in the crowd, who had caused a fair share of trouble. 'You, you, you – all of you – are here in my home. Most of you doing things in my home that you wouldn't dream of doing in your own home. How would you feel ...' He pointed an accusing finger at one lout, 'if we all went back to your home and tore down the curtains, or took the things down off the walls and just dropped them on the floor and kicked them to bits; or broke your windows and then casually said, "Let's go upstairs and kill the people up there"?'

'My parents aren't Vampires,' the lout shouted at Valentine.

'Mine neither,' Valentine whipped back. One or two people started to applaud. One man shouted:

'Well then, what do *you* think we should do?'

'I'll tell you,' Valentine said happily. 'I think I should go and have a talk with the King and see if I can't, on your behalf, talk him into abdicating the throne.'

'We don't want your brother to be our King,' a voice from the back sang out.

'And neither do I. But I also don't want him killed.' Valentine looked around at his captive audience. 'Listen to me. Who else can speak to them, the King and the Queen, other than me? The King treated me as his son. At least I know he will listen to me. But there is not one man here who he will listen to, nor is there anyone here brave enough to face him alone because you are petrified that he would cast some sort of spell on you. Am I right?' Valentine was getting quite excited and was beginning to enjoy himself.

'He won't put a curse on *me*, I will promise you that.'

Igon looked up at his friend and, not to be outdone, shouted, 'Hear! Hear!'

Valentine told the assembled group what he had in mind to say to the King. No half measures. It would take time but he felt sure that he could do it

and he should be given the opportunity to try. 'Let me go to the King now.'

Near the door a man shouted, 'That's the most sensible thing I've heard all evening.'

Everyone turned round to look at a rather handsome, blond man carrying a fresh loaf under his arm. He continued, 'Of course this man should go and talk to the King. He must. And if anyone here tries to stop him, or impede him in any way, remember this. In thirty more days I'll be a werewolf again and a werewolf with a good memory makes a bad enemy.'

Loud applause greeted this. Many people started to shout, 'Go and see the King.'

*   *   *

Vernon had been up and down the cellar steps eight times and had still not out-magicked his father. He had almost run out of verses, spells, ointments and breath. On his last trip back to the cellar he peeped through a curtain and listened to his brother shouting at the crowd but, joy upon joy, he had seen Igon and was now lying in wait for him.

As Valentine, followed by Igon, ran up the stairs to the unliving quarters of the King, he shouted to Igon to hurry but Igon couldn't hurry and was slowly and painfully climbing the stairs. His good friend Valentine shouted that he would see Igon in the King's chamber.

Behind a curtain Vernon watched and listened. He let Valentine go by, thinking to himself, 'I'll save him for later'. He was quite happy waiting for the luckless Igon.

Igon eventually reached the curtain which Vernon was hiding behind. Vernon pounced on Igon, knocking almost all of the breath out of him, and quickly dragged him to the cellar.

Valentine was so far ahead of Igon, that he didn't hear Igon's short, sharp scream, and carried on to the King's room. He knocked out of respect and habit before entering the room. Inside the room stood a rather dishevelled King, his face blackened and his clothes torn and smouldering.

'Father,' he said, 'What happened?'

'Hello, Valentine,' said a very tired and almost exhausted Victor. 'Ooh, nothink really. Just Vernon up to his tricks but I'm proud to say, Valentine, that I beat him.'

He allowed a small, self-satisfied smile to play around his lips. The Queen was holding the King by the throat very tenderly. She spoke to Valentine.

'Now, where have you been, you naughty boy? Daddy and I have been awfully worried.'

'I've been in the village and there are many things I've got to talk to you about. Both of you.'

Ronnoco got to his feet and weakly stumbled to the window for air. He tripped over the rim of the carpet, knocking himself out on the edge of the coffin table. He never even saw Valentine. He lay there and, as usual, was completely ignored.

Doctor Plump was in a state of nervous jitters, twitching and moving, dancing and swaying, to un-heard music.

*　　　*　　　*

Vernon had by this time put Igon in the cellar on the rack. He was now at the mixing stage; mixing one potion with another, and chuckling to himself as the mixtures came together to form a diabolical fluid that would change the already sad and pathetic life that Igon led, to an even more pathetic one.

'Igon, my friend, in a few moments I will have the potion ready for you to drink. After one swallow you will be a different man. Not quite as handsome as you are now, you beast.'

Vernon laughed, half to himself and two quarters to Fang and Bruce. 'I promise you it won't be painful . . . at first. After a little while you will feel numb. Not like you are now, dumb, but numb. And then a little dizziness maybe. Then the pain – slight at first. It will slowly take over your whole miserable body and you will feel the pain of the whole world.

Yet you will not be able to pass into the blackness of oblivion. No, my friend. You will feel the pain for days before you turn into stone. Yes, little friend, stone. And the most interesting thing is, you will not be able to move or speak. You will not be able to ask for help. And the best part is that you will feel the pain getting worse as the days go by. Oh, my friend, I have waited a long time for this moment . . .'

Igon lay there, thinking and wondering why, if Vernon was going to do all these horrible things to him, did he insist on calling him 'my friend'?

'Soon, Igon, the only thing that you will suffer will be pain.' Vernon worked faster and faster as he sang to himself.

*   *   *

Meanwhile Grabbo and Areta had entered the castle and asked for Valentine. They were told that he was with the King and Queen. Grabbo nodded.

Upstairs, Valentine had explained to Victor and Valeeta the situation they were now in. He also understood the magic power Victor had, and could use on them, but at the moment Victor had little, if any, power left. He'd used it all on the bat and, of course, on Vernon. He was now completely empty of magic.

Valentine knew this and played on it for the benefit of his arguments. The Queen was on Valentine's side, wanting her husband to retire and settle down in the country, near a graveyard if possible. Victor wasn't too sure. He felt he still had a lot left in him yet.

After many hours of talk the King, who was now exhausted, finally nodded his regal Vampire head in agreement. The agreement was that Valentine should become President and that Victor should be Advisor to the President. Vernon was to be put out of the country and no villagers were to be harmed.

Victor and the Queen also told Valentine that he wasn't kidnapped as a child. He was found on the front doorstep of the castle. He had been left to die of starvation and cold so they had taken him in, loving him and sheltering him from the trials and tribulations of a human life.

Never once had he been chastised for being naughty. As a matter of fact, he had been the perfect baby, not like Vernon who was sulky and bad-tempered.

In turn, Valentine then told them of his forthcoming marriage. The King, in his wisdom, asked how long he had known the girl. Valentine told him the truth; a few hours.

Victor looked at his son and said, 'Mine son, there is, in Englant, a famous sayink, "Marry in Hastings ant repent in Leicester".'

Valentine knew he still had to talk to the people and convince them that everything would be fine. He

120

felt confident that he could do that. He shook hands with the King and kissed his mother and left their presence with a low bow.

Outside the royal rooms he stood for a moment, trying to take in everything that had happened. 'I must tell Igon that he has no need to worry now about Vernon . . . But where is he?'

He went back to the castle hall, thinking he would probably see Igon still making his way slowly up the stairs, but he didn't. However, he was more than happy to see Areta waiting for him with her father.

He told all the assembled people what plans had been made and, except for a few little points, they all basically agreed. He asked about Igon but no-one had seen him since he left with Valentine and tried to follow him up the steps to see the King.

Valentine began to get worried. Of course, he knew that the King wouldn't harm Igon, not so soon after the agreement that they had just hammered out. So who else? Suddenly he knew. Vernon! That was it. Vernon had got him. He looked round and saw Wilf talking to Grabbo and Areta. He walked swiftly over to them and explained the situation.

'Well, that's what happened, I should say, Prime Minister,' Wilf said.

'President,' Grabbo corrected.

'It's all the same thing. Prime Minister, President, King,' retorted Wilf. The important thing is to see if we can find Igon. Let's go to the cellar first. I bet that's where Vernon has got him.'

*   *   *

While Valentine, Areta, Grabbo and Wilf were looking for their friend Igon, lower down, in the pit of the

121

castle, Vernon was busily and happily making his potions. Igon was thinking of what was going to become of him.

Upstairs, the King and Queen were packing their cases. Pretty soon it would be dawn and they would have to sleep the day through. The Queen looked at her husband with eyes full of love and admiration and said:

'Sweetness?'

'Yes, mine little moonpeam?' He smiled, putting his spare top hat in a tall case.

'I think you did the right thing. And I also think that Valentine will make a wonderful President. It's a pity about Vernon being a bit silly.'

'Ya. Valentine vill make a gut President,' Victor half smiled to himself. 'If he does as I'm tellink him.'

The Doctor had stopped moving and twitching. He was now wondering what was going to happen to him. Ronnoco came round at last. 'What happened?' he asked weakly.

'Nothink,' said the King. 'Vell, nothink that you vill notice. I vill still be in charge.' He spoke happily for the first time that week.

*   *   *

Valentine and his friends were still searching for Igon in every room that they could find but as yet not one had led them to their little friend.

'Keep trying,' Valentine pleaded to the others, but they were running out of cellars and rooms to search.

Then Valentine stopped suddenly in his tracks. 'Yes,' he shouted. 'Yes. That's where he'll be.'

'Where?' his friends asked.

'In the cellar almost in the bowels of the earth.'

122

'That one,' Wilf asked, 'that everybody says is only a few yards from Australia?'

'That's the one, Wilf.'

'Do you know the way?'

'I'm not sure,' Valentine said thoughtfully. 'I've never been there – Vernon has never invited me. Apart from the King and Queen, and of course Vernon himself, no-one has been there, and if they have, they've never been seen again.'

'Well, let's try and get there before it's too late,' said Grabbo.

'Follow me,' said Valentine, taking Areta's hand. Almost twenty minutes of fast walking found them outside a huge door made of the strongest wood with great iron bars across it.

Valentine gathered his friends around him and whispered, 'I would say, knowing Vernon, that there must be a secret way to get into this room. Or maybe a secret panel . . .'

His friends nodded. 'What shall we do?'

'Quietly push and pull every nail and panel you can see or even touch. It's bound to be here because, look . . .' He pointed to the door. 'There's no lock on this door. Please, everyone, don't lose heart. Think of poor Igon and the pain and worry he's going through.'

They all felt sad and with renewed energy worked as hard as they could.

The minutes ticked slowly by for them, and ticked quickly by for Igon. Then Areta let out a small cry. 'Look! This large screw. I don't think it's fastened to anything.'

'Let me see,' Valentine whispered. He carefully, with a finger, turned the screw.

'You're right, Areta. It doesn't seem to be attached to anything. Keep turning it.'

'Maybe it's like a safe. You know, so many turns to the left and then so many to the right,' Wilf said. As he spoke, Areta cupped her hand and caught the screw as it fell out. Inside where the screw had been was a tiny button.

'Shall I press it?' whispered Valentine.

'Of course you must, my Lord.' Wilf nodded.

'*President*,' Grabbo said.

'Oh, all right, President,' Wilf whispered loudly. 'What's it matter as long as it gets pressed.'

As Areta had the smallest finger, she pressed the button and they all listened, hardly daring to breathe. There was a slight whirring sound followed by a small click; a few seconds of silence, then another louder click and quite suddenly, and noiselessly, the door swung open beautifully, as smooth as silk. Vernon had made that door and it was a masterpiece of engineering.

Four pale and nervous faces peered round the door into a large room. They tentatively walked into the laboratory. Vernon had heard nothing above the noise of his singing and the bubbling and burping of his experiments.

Igon was still on the rack. The rescuing group looked at each other as if to say 'At least we're not too late.' Igon had his eye closed, not wanting to see Vernon mixing the potion that was to turn him into stone and everlasting pain. He thought of his Mummy and what she would have done to Vernon if she was here.

Vernon took a medicine drop and in it put some of the potion. He picked up a largish beetle from a box

124

and dropped a minute globule on to the beetle. He watched the beetle, a black one with things like horns protruding from the side of its head. It stopped moving as soon as the liquid touched it. That could, of course, be put down to reaction, as the beetle was not expecting it to rain. It moved forward after a second or two, then stopped mid-step, one of its horns held high, the other low. It also turned a stone-coloured grey.

Vernon picked it up. It was very hot and he dropped it quickly back on to the laboratory table. It bounced along the table, as would a dropped stone. Vernon smiled, grinned, laughed and then screamed for joy. 'It works,' he shouted.

Igon opened his eye and gulped.

'It works, Igon. Aren't you thrilled? Say you're thrilled, you magotty thing.'

Vernon showed him the stone beetle. Igon looked away.

The four friends crept as quietly as they could past tubes and boiling vats of what looked like coloured water. Vernon was thrilled with himself and the outcome of this experiment.

'You know, Igon, my friend,' he said, showing him a hammer and chisel. 'Within a few minutes you will be turned to stone and I will be able to sign my name on my work. Think of it, Igon. You're such a lucky fellow. I'm going to immortalise you.'

Igon moaned and turned his head away from Vernon. This time he turned it in the direction of his friends who were hiding behind the glass vats and the gurgling and bubbling phials, with their fingers over their mouths, silently telling Igon not to make a sound. Igon nodded to the best of his ability.

Vernon looked at Igon and thought that he was nodding to the fact that he was to be immortalised.

Valentine and the others crept forward as carefully as they could. The idea was to overpower Vernon and restrain him somehow, while Areta untied Igon. Then they were all to run like the wild bunch as fast as they could. Wilf and Grabbo would carry Igon because speed wasn't his best asset.

Vernon held up a large test tube in front of his eyes to measure the correct amount that was to go into the cup for Igon to drink. It had to be the exact measurement; a driblet too much and Igon would crack within a few hours; a driblet less and he wouldn't set. It had to be perfect.

While closely looking at the test tube, Vernon thought he saw a movement in the reflection. Although he couldn't see himself he could see the reflection of everything else. He saw four small figures, slowly making their way towards him. He knew them all except the girl. He thought quickly. If he put the test tube down he would be at a disadvantage, as he wouldn't then be able to see them without turning round, and if he turned round they would know that he could see them and the advantage was theirs.

No, he thought, the only thing to do was to let them advance, thinking they were unnoticed. Then, at the first opportunity, to throw the contents of the test tube on them. It would only need a touch and they would be stone within seconds. That way he would still have Igon to play with and also have a backing group for Igon to stand in front of when he put them all up in the market square. He was looking forward to the next few minutes.

127

Igon, whose eye kept going first to the group and then back to Vernon, at such an alarming rate that Areta feared it might drop out altogether, watched as his friends crept closer to each other, forming a group that looked pretty formidable. But Igon knew, as they all did, that Vernon was no fool.

Suddenly Vernon spoke.

'Good evening, Gentlemen and, of course, Lady. Welcome to my, er, workshop.' He kept his back to them. 'I wouldn't do anything silly, like rush me, because the mixture in this tube – well, the smallest drop and you are all turned to stone. Isn't that right, Igon? Tell them about the beetle, Igon.'

The four of them stopped and looked at Igon.

He nodded his head and said, 'It's true, Sire. That thing there, that looks like a stone. Well, five minutes ago it was a beetle and was walking along the top of the table. And it isn't dead. It's alive but it's stone. One drop of that stuff in the tube and you will be stone too, but not dead. Just pain for ever.'

'Thank you, Igon.' Vernon smiled with a coolness that was irritating. 'I couldn't have said it better myself, except to add that the pain lasts forever and it also gets worse every day. And, of course, you won't be able to speak or ask for help. Just suffer. May I say how nice it was of you to come here and, er, how shall I say . . . volunteer? To try out this formula.'

Wilf and Valentine started to move but Vernon laughed at them. 'I wouldn't come too close, Gentlemen. By the way, have you met my dog? Fang and Bruce.'

The two-headed dog growled from the darkness under the table and showed its heads with snarling teeth and four almost irridescent eyes.

'Stay!' he commanded the dog and it slunk back under the working table.

'There is nothing you can do. You might as well admit that you are now prisoners. My prisoners. And I must say how clever it was of you to find the screw in the door and open it.

But, as always, there is something you didn't think of. You see, when you came in, the door closed on itself and it can only be opened with a key of which there is only one and I am the only person who knows where it is. To be honest, and without wishing to sound conceited, don't you think I'm rather clever?' He turned towards them with his back resting against the table and the tube still in his hand.

He raised the tube to the level of his eyes. 'Look at it, Gentlemen, and you too, Miss. That's all it is. Just a little drop of white fluid that looks so harmless and yet can cause so much suffering.'

Grabbo held Areta close to him and felt her shiver with fright.

'So who's first then? What? No eager volunteers?' He looked round the group. No one moved. 'Oh, come now, Gentlemen. Do you want the lady to think she is consorting with cowards?' He grinned at them.

'What about you, dear brother? Everybody's favourite. Wouldn't you like to be made into stone and be immortalised for ever.' He held the test tube close up to his brother's face, making him step back.

'You, Grabbo the stupid publican?' He looked at Grabbo with contempt. 'Or your beautiful daughter?' He straightened up and took a small step towards them. They all backed off.

'Wilf? Oh yes, we mustn't forget Wilf, must we?

The footballing dog.' Then he looked at Igon. 'Don't worry, my friend.'

'For the last time, you mad, raving idiot, I am not your friend. I'm rather choosy whom I pick for my friends and you are certainly not one of them, you stupid, mad, sick oaf...'

Everybody thought that was Igon's last sentence on earth. Vernon was so taken aback that it gave Wilf the opportunity he had been waiting for. He had seen the rubber ball the dog had chased. It was now by his foot. He kicked it as hard as he could away from Vernon who was standing with his back to the table the dog was under. As the ball sped along the laboratory floor he shouted, 'Fang! Bruce! Fetch.'

The dog shot out from under the table at an

incredible speed and ran between Vernon's legs, knocking him and the test tube up in the air. The fluid came down on him and he was stone almost before he could scream. Before their eyes, Vernon turned the colour of a Cotswold cottage. The dog came back and dropped the ball in Vernon's out-stretched hand. It melted.

Valentine held Areta in his arms as Grabbo re-leased Igon from the rack. Wilf poured a vat of water over Vernon to cool him off, then picked him up and carried him to the door with the help of Grabbo and Igon. Valentine looked at the dog and round one of its necks, attached to the collar, was a key. He spoke gently to them and tentatively put a hand out towards the collar.

Fang growled and Bruce tried to lick it.

'Where's your lead then?' The heads ran to the door and jumped up to the hanging lead.

'Walkies,' Valentine said loudly. The dog sat down, perfectly still and allowed Valentine to take the key from its collar. He unlocked the door and all of them left the cellar, including the two-headed dog.

Within a few days the official Presidential Election took place, making Valentine the first ever President of Gotcha.

CHAPTER 9

King Victor retires: 'It's time I was gone.'
But the biggest surprise comes to Igon.

The abdication of King Victor and Queen Valeeta took place in style. The King made a speech and showed a piece of magic that made the Gotchas very happy and one man in particular.

The King and his Queen stood on the balcony of the castle and looked down on the thousands of people that had travelled from far and wide to be there. The King raised his arms and started to speak. The crowd were still.

'Mine people. Or maybe I should say mine ex-people. Or maybe I should say mine friends.' Loud, long cheers followed that statement. 'Today is both a joyful ant a sad day for me. Sad, because I'm givink up beink your Kink. Ant joyful, because mine adopted son, Valentine, is takink over the rulink off you. He is goink to be your President ant if he vants any advice, then let him come to me. But before mine vife ant I leave you, may I do somethink that I should haff done many years ago ant I am ashamed that I didn't think off it then.'

He beckoned to Igon to step forward. He was lifted on to a table so the whole of the Kingdom – or the country – could see him. Igon waved to the people below. The cheers were enormous.

Victor continued. 'Many bad thinks haff been done to this poor, unfortunate man. A man who could not help beink born the vay he vos. I am sad to say this, but even I haff done bad thinks to this little man vithout thinkink vether I haff hurt his feelinks or not. I vould now like to make up for the bad thinks that all of us haff done to Igon.'

The King held Igon close to him. Igon blinked his one eye, not knowing very much about what was going on; only happy to be there. The King drew a deep breath. He held Igon even tighter till Igon could feel the breath leaving his body. He also realised that there was no breath coming back into his body. He tried hard to breathe but he couldn't. A minute later he had fainted.

The crowd began to get a little worried, thinking that the King was playing some devilish trick and that Igon was dead. Then the King slowly, and with great care, laid Igon on the table. The murmuring swelled louder.

Suddenly the King pointed his long fingers at the still body of Igon and as he did so it was covered in thick, white smoke. The King concentrated very hard, the blue veins bulging along his forehead and neck. The smoke suddenly cleared, as quickly as if a

gale had blown it away. There was a gasp from the crowd. Igon was no longer there, but in his place, was the most handsome of men.

The King helped lift the new Igon to his feet. He stood there, looking down at the crowd, in the same place that he had been only a minute before. But now Igon was wearing the most beautiful white military suit. He was six feet tall, broad as a house and with two of the most wonderful blue eyes. Tears were running down both cheeks.

The King spoke again. 'My friends. May I, as my last gift as your Kink, giff you Igon. No ... Prince Igon of Gotcha.'

The crowd cheered, the President and his wife clapped their approval and the Queen moved towards Prince Igon and kissed him on both cheeks.

Igon waved to all his friends, shook hands with the King, and left the balcony. As he walked into the inner room he almost slipped. He looked down and saw a bright blue marble lying on the floor. He felt where his pouch would have been. It was still there. It was empty. He bent down and with a smile rubbed the marble against his sleeve and held it up to the light saying. 'You won't have to cry now,' and put it back in its pouch.

*   *   *

Valentine and Areta were married and he made a first class President. Wilf became the Gotcha football team's manager and would have got them to the World Cup except for the fact that they lost their first match so were knocked out of the competition.

Grabbo opened the largest hotel in Gotcha by the River Armenleg. He called it the Hotel Gotcha by the

Arm and Leg. Doctor Plump was given a special job.
He became the Number One Doctor to the President's horse.

King Victor and his Queen settled down in the
country, close to the village of Katchem and more or
less became the Squire and his Lady. They are fortunately still alive and very happy and if you visit the
land of Gotcha they are always thrilled if you call in
on them.

If you do visit this land then you must make your
way to the park and have a look at the statues. There's
one in particular that, so the children say, on very
cold days, if you put your ear against it, you can hear
little cries of 'Help...help...' But fortunately for
Vernon, Vampires can feel no pain. The only feeling
Vernon had was that one day he would be back. Who
knows..?

A Selected List of Fiction from Mammoth

While every effort is made to keep prices low, it is sometimes necessary to increase prices at short notice. Mammoth Books reserves the right to show new retail prices on covers which may differ from those previously advertised in the text or elsewhere.

The prices shown below were correct at the time of going to press.

☐	416 13972 8	**Why the Whales Came**	Michael Murpurgo	£2.50
☐	7497 0034 3	**My Friend Walter**	Michael Murpurgo	£2.50
☐	7497 0035 1	**The Animals of Farthing Wood**	Colin Dann	£2.99
☐	7497 0136 6	**I Am David**	Anne Holm	£2.50
☐	7497 0139 0	**Snow Spider**	Jenny Nimmo	£2.50
☐	7497 0140 4	**Emlyn's Moon**	Jenny Nimmo	£2.25
☐	7497 0344 X	**The Haunting**	Margaret Mahy	£2.25
☐	416 96850 3	**Catalogue of the Universe**	Margaret Mahy	£1.95
☐	7497 0051 3	**My Friend Flicka**	Mary O'Hara	£2.99
☐	7497 0079 3	**Thunderhead**	Mary O'Hara	£2.99
☐	7497 0219 2	**Green Grass of Wyoming**	Mary O'Hara	£2.99
☐	416 13722 9	**Rival Games**	Michael Hardcastle	£1.99
☐	416 13212 X	**Mascot**	Michael Hardcastle	£1.99
☐	7497 0126 9	**Half a Team**	Michael Hardcastle	£1.99
☐	416 08812 0	**The Whipping Boy**	Sid Fleischman	£1.99
☐	7497 0033 5	**The Lives of Christopher Chant**	Diana Wynne-Jones	£2.50
☐	7497 0164 1	**A Visit to Folly Castle**	Nina Beechcroft	£2.25

All these books are available at your bookshop or newsagent, or can be ordered direct from the publisher. Just tick the titles you want and fill in the form below.

Mandarin Paperbacks, Cash Sales Department, PO Box 11, Falmouth, Cornwall TR10 9EN.

Please send cheque or postal order, no currency, for purchase price quoted and allow the following for postage and packing:

UK   80p for the first book, 20p for each additional book ordered to a maximum charge of £2.00.

BFPO   80p for the first book, 20p for each additional book.

Overseas   £1.50 for the first book, £1.00 for the second and 30p for each additional book
including Eire   thereafter.

NAME (Block letters) ....

ADDRESS ....

....

....